Hidden in the broom cupboard of
Rose Cottage is the most delightful little
house. Shh, it's a secret. No one knows
it's there ... This is the home of
Tumtum and Nutmeg ...

When General Marchmouse runs
away in Arthur's toy bus, he gets a big
surprise. A circus has arrived in the
meadow! But there's more to this
travelling troupe than meets the eye,
and soon he finds the village
policemouse on his tail.

Also by Emily Bearn

Tumtum & Nutmeg
A CIRCUS ADVENTURE

by Emily Bearn

Illustrated by Nick Price

EGMONT

Praise for Tumtum & Nutmeg

'Told simply, with charming detail, this old-fashioned and well-published story . . . will delight children who are of an age to relish secret friends and a cosy world in miniature.' *Sunday Times*

'Bearn is a fine writer and her tale . . . is a gently humorous page-turner full of little details . . . Highly recommended.' *Financial Times*

'This is most definitely a candidate for a classic of the future.' LoveReading4Kids

'Bearn's style is as crisp and warm as a home-baked biscuit.' Amanda Craig, *The Times*

'I bought this to give to my god-daughter . . . but wanting to make sure it was suitable I checked by reading the first few pages. I can only say it was glued to my hand until two hours later when I'd reached the end . . . Old-fashioned in the best sense of the word, it's charmingly illustrated and a wonderful story.' *The Oldie*

'A timeless book: charming, witty, intelligent, gentle, kind, and extremely exciting. Like E.B. White with a spider in *Charlotte's Web*, Emily Bearn has taken those little-loved creatures, mice, and made them adorable and compelling . . . I'd recommend this to all parents of children of reading age.' Amazon

'A wonderfully sweet and charmingly illustrated novel for younger readers which put me in mind of the *Brambly Hedge* stories . . . This is a warm and gentle story.' Askews Library Service

'This is a brilliant engaging story full of wonderful characters.' *Primary Times*

'This is an extremely well-written book that reminds me of Beatrix Potter. The illustrations are superb.' writeaway.org.uk

'Gentle humour and old-fashioned wisdom combine to create an instant classic that will be loved for years to come.' *Evening Express Aberdeen*

EGMONT

We bring stories to life

A Circus Adventure
First published 2010
by Egmont UK Limited
239 Kensington High Street, London W8 6SA

Text copyright © 2010 Emily Bearn
Cover and inside illustrations copyright © 2010 Nick Price

The moral rights of the author and illustrator have been asserted

ISBN 978 1 4052 5444 1

3 5 7 9 10 8 6 4 2

www.egmont.co.uk

A CIP catalogue record for this title is available
from the British Library

Typeset by Avon DataSet Ltd, Bidford on Avon, Warwickshire
Printed and bound in Great Britain by the CPI Group

*For Great
Aunt Daphne*

Chapter One

General Marchmouse swaggered past the compost heap, with a song rising in his heart. He had good reason to be cheerful. For today was his birthday! And mice do not have nearly as many birthdays as we do, so it was a very special day indeed.

He had been busy since breakfast time, opening his cards and unwrapping his presents.

And now it was almost dark, but the best part of the day was about to come. For tonight his friends Tumtum and Nutmeg had invited him for a birthday feast at Nutmouse Hall.

Perhaps Nutmeg will have made an earwig pie, he thought hungrily. *And a toad-in-the-hole, and a cockroach soufflé, and a strawberry trifle with toasted almonds on top!*

He hurried on under the rose bushes, and clambered down on to the garden path, with his invitation clutched tight in his paw.

It was a cold November evening, and he was glad to see Rose Cottage looming ahead of him. The curtains were still open, and all the windows were brightly lit.

'Hmm. It looks like the Mildews are at home,'

the General muttered. 'I shall have to be very careful – Tumtum will be furious if I give his hiding place away.'

He crept up to the back door, then wriggled under it and peeked his nose into the kitchen. There was a spider dozing on the doormat, and a cockroach scuttling beneath the sink. But there were no humans in sight. So he set off across the floor.

The General had visited Nutmouse Hall many times before, so he knew just where to go. It was a very grand house, built inside the Mildews' broom cupboard. And its front gates were hidden beneath the old wooden dresser that stood against the kitchen wall.

The General marched along, taking his usual route – past the laundry basket, under the vegetable

rack, then round the leg of the kitchen table.

He hadn't far to go, and when he peered under the dresser he could see a tiny bead of light coming from the Nutmouses' gates. He hurried on, wading through a puddle of ketchup on the floor.

But then suddenly he stepped into a dark shadow. And when he looked up, he saw the most astonishing sight:

It was a circus top!

The General froze, and stared at it in astonishment. It was the finest circus top he had ever seen. It had red and blue stripes, and it was bigger than a beach ball. And standing beside it was a little ticket booth with velvet curtains.

The General felt his heart quicken. *It must be*

a mouse circus, he thought, *for everything is mouse sized! Well, whomever it belongs to is a very lucky mouse, that's for sure!*

He stood there a moment, gazing admiringly at the big top. He wondered if there were dancing dragonflies or racing slugs inside, or any of the other wonderful things that mouse circuses usually have.

He decided to go in and see. But when he reached the entrance, he saw a silver card lying on the ground, with the words

written on the front.

'Well I never!' the General said. 'This circus

must be a present for me!'

The birthday card was bigger than he was. He heaved it open, wondering who it was from. But when he read what it said, his face fell:

Dear Arthur

This is a toy circus that I was given long ago, when I was not much older than you are now. I hope you enjoy playing with it as much as I did.

Happy birthday!

Love from Uncle Jeremy.

'Humph!' the General grunted. 'It must be Arthur's birthday too. So it's not a mouse circus after all – it's just a toy!'

The General thought it very unfair that the circus should have been given to Arthur instead of

him. 'It's far too good for a boy!' he said crossly.

He was still curious to see what was inside the big top. So he pulled open the flap, and marched through. And how he stared! For he had entered an enormous stadium, with tiered seats around the edges, and a trapeze up above. And before him was a huge throng of circus animals – wooden horses and leopards, and tigers and elephants, all prancing round the ring.

The General rubbed his eyes in astonishment. The toys looked so real, that for a moment he thought they were! And standing in their midst was a toy ringmaster, dressed in a shining gold suit, and holding a whip.

'Lucky fellow!' the General muttered. How he wished that he had a gold suit too! What fun it would be to stand in the middle of the ring, making the toy animals dance to the crack of his whip!

He stood there a long time, filled with envy. From somewhere in Rose Cottage, he heard the clock chime seven. He knew Tumtum and Nutmeg would be wondering where he was, for he was late for supper. And yet he couldn't tear himself away.

'Surely there can't be any harm in my just trying the suit on and having one tiny crack of the whip,' he reasoned. 'It is my birthday, after all!'

He glanced guiltily over his shoulder. And after a very short period of hesitation, he marched up to the ringmaster and tore off his clothes. He tugged off his own Royal Mouse Army uniform, and tossed it to the floor. Then he pulled on the gold trousers. They were very tight, and he had to take a big breath in order to do up the button. But the jacket was a perfect fit.

He strutted about the ring, feeling very grand.

Then he snatched the whip, and gave it a hard crack. 'March!' he shouted. The lions shook, and an elephant toppled to the floor. The General whooped with joy – oh, what fun!

On he went, swaggering and shouting and cracking his whip, until soon all the wooden animals had been thrashed to the ground. No creature was spared. An elephant's trunk snapped off, and one of the lions lost a leg.

The General wondered what to do next.

Then he had a daring plan. *I know!* he thought. *I shall go and catch that cockroach I saw scuttling off*

under the sink, and train it to swing on the trapeze!

He tucked the whip under his arm, and ran out of the tent. But as he stepped into the kitchen, he got a terrible fright. Arthur and Lucy had appeared!

The General gulped, and dived back inside the big top. He had been making such a racket he hadn't heard them come downstairs. He knew that Arthur would be furious if he found him here, and saw what he had done to his toys.

He stood trembling, listening to the children's feet thudding on the floor.

'Just look at my circus!' Arthur said proudly. 'Isn't it the most splendid circus you've ever seen! I don't mind one bit that Pa forgot my birthday – this circus makes up for everything. Come on, let's play with it again.'

'All right,' Lucy replied. 'Wait a second while I put the milk bottles out.'

The General's mind whirled with terror. He heard Lucy open the garden door, and clank the bottles outside. Then he saw the children's shadows looming over the tent . . . There was nowhere he could hide . . .

There was a rustle, then the flap of the tent slowly opened, and a huge pink hand reached inside . . .

'Oh, what am I to do!' the General quivered. 'It's my birthday, and I'm going to be caught!'

But the General was a very lucky mouse. For at that very moment, as if by a miracle, the telephone rang.

'I bet that's Uncle Jeremy, calling to check the circus has arrived!' Arthur said.

The children both jumped up, and ran into the hall.

The General seized his chance to escape. In his haste, he forgot all about his army uniform, and dashed out of the big top wearing the ringmaster's clothes. Then he turned and hurtled towards Nutmouse Hall.

But as he skirted round the big top, he saw something so completely, utterly dazzling that for a moment it made him forget his fear. It was a bus. But not just any bus. This was, quite simply, the most splendid, most beautiful bus the General had *ever* seen.

It was gleaming red, with grinning headlights,

and silver wheels the size of saucers. He crept up to it, and pressed his nose to the window. There was a fat leather steering wheel, and a gear stick as big as a lollipop. And in the back of the bus were two little camp beds, with green quilts and crisp white pillows.

The General's whiskers twitched. The bus looked very inviting. He could hear Arthur and Lucy talking on the telephone in the hall. He knew they might come back into the kitchen at any moment, but he was too excited to care.

Then suddenly he felt a cold breeze cutting his ankles; and when he looked round he saw to his surprise that the children had left the garden door open.

He stood there a moment, peering out. The sky

14

had turned black, but he could see the pale outline of the garden path, twisting away in the moonlight.

And suddenly it was as if the moon and the stars were all calling out to him, whispering his name.

With a pounding heart, he pulled open the bus door and clambered into the driver's seat, tossing the whip in beside him. Then he gripped hold of the steering wheel, and flicked on the ignition.

The engine gave a shudder, then a *Vrooom!* and the bus shot forwards across the floor.

'Faster! Faster!' the General cried, slamming his paw on the accelerator. He swerved under the kitchen table, and tore towards the open door.

The spider fled out of his way, and a fly

splattered on the windscreen. The General clung tight to his seat as the bus bounced over the doorstep, and crashed on to the garden path. Then, with a shriek of joy, he turned on his headlights, and sped into the night.

Chapter Two

Nutmeg had been bustling and baking all afternoon, preparing the General's birthday feast. While she worked, Tumtum dozed in the library. When everything was nearly ready, he woke up and pottered into the kitchen, hoping to find a spoon to lick.

'Isn't it a coincidence that Arthur and the General have a birthday on the very same day?' he

said, dipping his paw into one of Nutmeg's mixing bowls.

'Yes, isn't it!' Nutmeg agreed. 'Oh, Tumtum, wouldn't it be lovely if Arthur could come to the birthday feast too! For you can be quite sure there shan't be any feasting going on in Rose Cottage. I peeked out into the kitchen earlier this afternoon, and there was no sign of a cake!'

'Are the children having something special for supper?' Tumtum asked.

'I shouldn't think so,' Nutmeg replied sadly. 'When I last looked in their larder, there was nothing except a stale loaf of bread, and a few tins of spaghetti!'

Tumtum wrinkled his nose. He had tried tinned spaghetti once, and he had not liked it at all.

It was a great mystery to him how humans could bear to eat it.

'Yes, it's a pity the children are too big to fit through our mouse-hole,' he agreed. 'Just think how astonished they would be if they could see all the delicious things *we* have to eat!'

'Well, at least Arthur got a nice birthday present,' Nutmeg said, briskly rolling her pastry.

'Did he?' Tumtum asked in surprise. 'Was it from his father?'

'Oh, gracious no! You know Mr Mildew never remembers about presents!' Nutmeg said. 'It was from his Uncle Jeremy – you remember, the nice old fellow we all went to stay with last summer at the seaside. He sent Arthur a beautiful toy circus; I saw it when I went out this afternoon. Arthur's

thrilled with it! I heard him telling Lucy that it was the best present he'd ever had!'

'Oh, I am glad,' Tumtum said, looking very relieved. It would have spoiled his appetite to think of Arthur having no presents as well as no cake. Now he could enjoy tonight's feast all the more.

'Now let's see,' Nutmeg said, rubbing her hands on her apron. 'I've still got to toast the croutons for the soup, and ice the cake, and glaze the ham, and chill the jellies, and warm the cockroach pasties . . . Then I think we're all done!'

'Goodness, what a lot of food we have,' Tumtum said. 'It's enough to feed a hundred mice! But there will only be three of us, now that Mrs Marchmouse can't come.'

'Yes, it is a rotten shame that she can't be

here,' Nutmeg sighed. 'But it's good of her to go and look after her sister. Apparently she's been very poorly. Mrs Marchmouse will probably have to stay with her for some time.'

'Well, I shouldn't think the General will mind being left on his own,' Tumtum said. 'You know what he's like. He loves getting into trouble, but it's not so easy when Mrs Marchmouse is watching over him!'

They both smiled. Mrs Marchmouse had been keeping a very strict eye on the General of late. He would probably consider a few days on his own a nice birthday treat!

'Well I shall make jolly sure that he doesn't get into trouble when he comes here,' Nutmeg said firmly. 'I'm not having him dragging us into

another adventure.'

'Certainly not,' Tumtum agreed. 'We've had quite enough of those! But you needn't worry, dear. The General will be much too busy eating to get up to any of his silly games. The only trouble he's likely to encounter tonight is indigestion!'

Nutmeg laughed. And as she put the finishing touches to all her little dishes, she felt full of warm feelings. Tumtum was right; there would be no adventures tonight. Just lots of fun and hearty eating!

'Gracious!' Nutmeg exclaimed, looking at the clock. 'He'll be here soon, and we still haven't laid the table!'

They both hurried through to the banqueting room, and lit all the candles. Then they laid the

24

table with their best silver and china, for today was a very special occasion.

When everything was ready, they went upstairs to change. Nutmeg put on her pink dress, and Tumtum wore his velvet jacket. Then they settled down in the library, and waited for the General to arrive.

But the time ticked by, and the clock struck seven – and still he did not appear.

'I hope he hasn't got lost,' Nutmeg fussed.

'Oh, no, he knows the way much too well for that,' Tumtum said. 'He's probably just stopped to chase a beetle. You know what he's like!'

But Nutmeg still felt anxious. For it was unlike the General to be late for a meal.

They sat there a little longer, nervously

sipping their champagne. Then suddenly they heard raised voices coming from the Mildews' kitchen. It was Arthur and Lucy, and they sounded very upset.

Tumtum and Nutmeg could hear everything that was being said:

'But where is it? It can't just have gone!' Arthur cried.

'Well I haven't taken it,' Lucy said.

'Well you must have, no one else has been in here today!' Arthur shouted.

'No I haven't!' Lucy said crossly. 'Why would I want to take your silly circus bus? I tell you, I haven't touched it.'

'But you *must* have taken it,' Arthur wailed. 'I left it here, by the big top. It can't just have vanished

26

into thin air!'

Tumtum and Nutmeg looked at each other in surprise. They knew all the comings and goings at Rose Cottage, and no one else had been there today.

'Arthur must be mistaken – no one could have taken the bus,' Nutmeg said. 'It was certainly there when I went out earlier, and I know no one's been in the kitchen since then . . . except –'

The mice looked at each other and gulped. For the same thought had entered both their minds.

'Oh, Tumtum,' Nutmeg whispered. 'You don't think . . . I mean . . . you don't really think . . . Oh, *surely* the General couldn't have been wicked enough to steal Arthur's bus!?'

Chapter Three

Tumtum and Nutmeg hurried out of Nutmouse Hall, and tiptoed to the edge of the dresser. They could see Arthur kneeling on the floor, his head lowered as he peered into the big top.

'Someone's knocked over all the animals,' he cried. 'And look – they've broken my wooden elephant, *and* one of the lions!'

He turned round, and glared at his sister. 'It

must have been you!' he shouted, holding up the broken toys for her to see. 'Who else could have done it?'

'Oh, don't be so horrid!' Lucy said. 'I told you, I didn't touch your circus. I haven't been near it all day!'

Arthur scowled, but he knew Lucy was telling the truth. She wouldn't have broken his toys; she wasn't that sort of sister.

'Let me look inside,' Lucy said, for she could see that he was very upset. Arthur shuffled aside, then Lucy knelt down in front of the big top and peeked in. And she noticed something very strange. 'Look!' she said. 'Someone's taken the ringmaster's clothes!' She reached in through the flap, and pulled the toy out of the tent. And when Arthur saw it he was amazed. When he had last played with it, it had been wearing a gold suit. But while he had been gone, someone had stripped it to its underpants!

'Hang on, here are some other clothes!' Lucy exclaimed, spotting the tiny garments that the General had tossed to the floor. She plucked them out, and spread them on the palm of her hand. The children looked at them curiously.

'Look at these tiny gold medals on the jacket!' Arthur said. 'It looks like an army uniform. But it's not like the uniform a toy soldier would have. It seems too . . . well . . . *too real*!'

Lucy agreed. 'And isn't this strange,' she said, pointing to the jacket. 'There are hairs on the collar! This can't belong to a toy. It must belong to

something real.'

'Whoever he is, he must have crept in here when we weren't looking, then changed into the ringmaster's clothes and driven away in the bus!'

It was very mysterious, and the children were longing to find out who the secretive creature could be.

'Come on, let's find him!' Arthur said, running to grab the torch from the shelf by the back door. 'The bus was still here when the telephone rang, so he can't have got far!'

Tumtum and Nutmeg were still crouched under the dresser. They watched in dismay as the children raced outside.

'So it *was* him!' Nutmeg said. 'And to think

that he even stole the ringmaster's clothes! Oh, Tumtum! How could he be so silly? And now the children are sure to catch him, and lock him up in a cage!'

'It serves him right if they do,' Tumtum said crossly. 'Really, what a fool he's been!'

'But just think how upset Mrs Marchmouse will be when she comes home and we have to tell her the General's been taken prisoner,' Nutmeg said anxiously. 'You remember how upset she was when it happened before!'

The children had once caught the General playing in their doll's house, and they had taken him to school with them, and put him in a cage full of pet gerbils. Mrs Marchmouse had been quite distraught.

Tumtum sighed. Nutmeg was right, it would be too awful if Mrs Marchmouse had to go through that again.

'Let's see what's going on outside,' he said. They crept over to the back door, and peered anxiously into the garden.

The children were rushing back and forth, beaming the torch round the lawn and the flower beds.

'Come on! It must be here somewhere,' Arthur cried.

They searched high and low – round the vegetable patch, and the dustbins, and the compost heap – but the bus wasn't there.

'I don't understand it!' Arthur groaned. 'It can't just have vanished!'

34

'We'll have to come and look again in the morning,' Lucy said. 'It's too dark now.'

'All right,' Arthur agreed, for they had been outside for ages, and his hands were turning numb with cold. 'But I can tell you, whoever the thief is, he'll be sorry when I catch him!'

Tumtum and Nutmeg crouched behind the bootjack while Arthur and Lucy walked back inside. They did not speak until the children had gone upstairs.

'Well, I'm glad they didn't catch him – Arthur sounded very cross!' Nutmeg said. 'But where can he be? They've looked everywhere!'

'He must have gone further afield,' Tumtum said. 'I'll bet he's driven down into the meadow! You know how much he loves to go exploring

there, and just think how much fun he could have in a bus!'

'Oh, dear. You're probably right,' Nutmeg said anxiously. She hadn't thought of the meadow. It was below Rose Cottage, and it was a wild place. It had a stream running along the bottom, and at night it was full of foxes. Tumtum was right; the General loved to go adventuring there. 'I hope he doesn't come to any harm,' she said.

'Oh, he'll be all right inside his bus,' Tumtum said. 'And you can be quite sure, he'll turn up as soon as he's hungry. He won't want to miss his birthday feast! Now come on, we'd better get home in case the children come downstairs again.'

They hurried across the kitchen, and let themselves back into Nutmouse Hall. They were no longer in the mood for champagne. So Nutmeg made a pot of tea, and they sat by the fire waiting for the General's familiar *Rap! Tap! Tap!* at the door.

But the hours slipped by, and when ten o'clock struck he still hadn't appeared.

Nutmeg was very fussed.

'I shouldn't worry, dear; he's probably just decided to camp out for the night,' Tumtum said, trying to raise her spirits. 'You know how he can't resist an adventure. We might as well get some sleep, then we can set out and look for him first thing in the morning.'

Nutmeg agreed, for after her long day of baking and worrying, she felt very tired. And the house felt sad now that their party had been

spoiled. So they blew out the candles in the banqueting room, and climbed upstairs to bed.

But if they could only have seen what their friend was getting up to, they would not have slept a wink that night. For the General had fallen into a much bigger adventure than he had planned.

Chapter Four

The General drove so fast, it is no wonder the children hadn't been able to find him. After leaving the cottage he had sped straight to the far end of the garden, then slipped underneath the tall farm gate into the meadow.

He heard an owl hoot and a fox howl, but he felt not a whit of fear. The night was his, and his whole body throbbed for adventure.

The General knew just where he wanted to go. He would drive all the way to the bottom of the meadow, and spend the night camping by the stream! The grass was taller than the bonnet of his bus, and the ground was rough. But he pressed on the accelerator, and bumped along as fast as he could, plotting his adventure.

Tonight he would ambush a snoozing snail, and roast it for his supper. And tomorrow morning he would catch a beetle, and make it trot round in circles to the crack of his whip. Then he'd put up a sign saying 'General Marchmouse's Circus Troupe', and invite all the field mice to his first show!

In his mind's eye, he saw himself strutting about in his gold suit, showing off to the crowd, and he felt a lovely warm glow in his stomach.

What a glorious adventure it promised to be! But adventures cannot be planned, as the General was about to discover.

For just as he was coming within sight of the stream, he saw something that made him start. A little way off along the bank, there was a cluster of bright lights! On spotting them he quickly stopped, and turned off his engine, wondering what they could be.

At first he could not see much, for the moon had been swallowed by a cloud. But a few moments later the cloud scudded in the breeze, and a thin shaft of light shone through, and spilled along the bank. The General sat back in his seat with a jolt. For he could see now where the lights were coming from, and he could hardly believe it.

For lo and behold if it wasn't another circus – with wooden wagons and a big top! But this circus was no toy. It was a *real live* mouse circus, there could be no mistake of that. They had a snail roasting on their campfire, and the General could see four mice silhouetted against the tent.

He was *furious*. He couldn't set up his own circus now: this one would steal all his business! There hadn't been a mouse circus visiting the village for ages. It was just his luck than one should show up now.

'I can't let them spoil my adventure. I shall go and tell them to buzz off!' he decided. He grabbed his whip, and slid out of the bus. Then off he marched towards the big top, grinding his teeth.

44

The circus was surrounded by a low fence, lit with lanterns. And at the entrance there was a wooden booth with a sign saying

The General rapped on the window, but there was no reply. He rapped again. Then he barged through the gate.

He looked about him in surprise. For the circus did not look nearly so impressive from the inside. The ground was strewn with litter, and the big top was full of holes.

The circus mice were sitting round their campfire, eating roasted flies. When they saw the General they all looked up and snarled.

45

The General was taken aback, for the mice looked rather sinister.

There were four of them, and they all had fiery red fur and piercing black eyes. One was as thin as a pipe cleaner and had a scar on his nose. He was dressed in a scarlet suit, and was clearly the ringmaster. And the other three were dressed as clowns, but somehow they did not look at all as clowns should. Their mouths turned down at the corners, and their fangs were dark yellow.

'What are you doing here?' the ringmaster snarled.

'I've come to tell you to buzz off!' the General replied rudely. 'There is only room for one circus in this meadow and . . .'

But before he could get any further, one of

the clowns walked up and gave him a shove. 'Who do you think you are, telling us to buzz off!' he shouted. '*You* buzz off! Go on, *SHOO!*'

The others had gathered behind him, looking at the General with menace. But the General was too cross to feel afraid: 'How dare you! Do you know who I am!' he raged. 'I am the Great General Marchmouse, and I warn you now, if you mess with me you will have the Royal Mouse Army to answer to!'

His words had a powerful effect. General Marchmouse was a very famous name in the mouse community, and the circus mice were clearly impressed.

The ringmaster gave a cold smile. And when he spoke, his voice sounded quite different. It was

48

almost a simper:

'General Marchmouse! This *is* an honour, to be sure! Will you stay and share our pan-roasted flies?'

The General was flustered by the ringmaster's sudden change in tone. It struck him that his voice sounded false. But the flies did smell very delicious, and it seemed ages since he had last eaten.

'Well, all right then, I suppose I might have time for a quick bite,' he said, eyeing the frying pan greedily.

One of the clowns handed him a plate, and they all sat down round the campfire. Once he had started munching his fly, the General felt quite chatty.

'Tell me, are you new to these parts?' he

asked. 'It's ages since we last had a circus in the meadow.'

'We just arrived here this afternoon,' one of the clowns replied. 'And we're doing our first show tomorrow. All the field mice are coming. We're nearly sold out.'

'Gracious!' the General said. 'And where are you all from?'

'Oh, we're town mice!' the ringmaster replied grandly. 'I used to belong to the Red Top Circus, but I left a few months ago to set up on my own.'

The General looked at him in amazement. 'The Red . . . Y-you mean to say . . . *Good grief!*'

The General was very impressed. For the Red Top Circus was the most popular circus in the

whole land. Mice travelled for miles to see its giant beetles and its dancing dragonflies and its racing slugs. As a schoolmouse, the General had saved his pocket money to see their shows, and had known the names of all the performers.

'Well I'm blessed!' he said.

The ringmaster looked very pleased. 'Master Goldtail's my name,' he said, 'and these are my clowns – Mr Merry, Mr Mirth, and Mr Moody.'

Everyone shook paws. 'Goldtail, *Goldtail* . . .' the General said, racking his brains.

'Yes, yes . . . I'm sure I remember your name!' he said uncertainly. 'Were you one of the trapeze mice, who shot out of a cannon?'

'That's right,' Master Goldtail said quickly. 'I was one of the best trapeze mice they'd ever had.

But I wanted to be a ringmaster, so I left Red Top and set up on my own!'

'Good for you,' the General said admiringly. He had been very cross to find another circus in the meadow; but he felt quite differently now he knew whose circus it was.

'I must buy a ticket to your show,' he said, scrabbling in his pocket. But then his face fell: 'Oh, drat,' he muttered. 'My wallet's in my jacket pocket – and I left my jacket in Arthur's big top!'

'Arthur's big top?' Master Goldtail asked anxiously. 'But I haven't heard of Arthur's Circus. I thought *we* were the only mouse circus in these parts.'

'Oh, Arthur's Circus isn't a mouse circus!' the General laughed. And then he told them the

whole story of his adventure so far – about how he had stumbled across a toy circus at Rose Cottage, and stolen the ringmaster's gold suit, and sped off in the shiny red bus before anyone could catch him.

Master Goldtail and his clowns hooted admiringly. They thought it very funny. No one showed any disapproval.

'There's my bus, over there,' the General said proudly, pointing through the grass. 'She's goes as fast as a hare – and she's got a horn and camp beds and real leather seats!'

The others all turned to look. And when they saw the big red bus gleaming in the moonlight, their jaws dropped in surprise.

No one said a word. The General could see

they were very envious.

'Where's your bus?' he asked, feeling rather superior.

'We don't have one,' Master Goldtail replied. 'We had a squirrel to tow our wagons, but she escaped when we were unloading this morning, and now she's disappeared up one of these trees. It's a wretched nuisance. We want to move on after tomorrow's show, but we won't be able to go anywhere until we've caught another squirrel, and that could take weeks!'

The General pondered this. Then, because he was feeling star struck, he made rather a rash suggestion:

'I say,' he said. 'Why don't you borrow my bus? I'm sure Arthur wouldn't mind if you took it for a day or two – and in return you can give me a ticket for tomorrow's show!'

The mice all looked very pleased.

'That's most kind of you,' Master Goldtail said, his eyes glinting greedily.

Then he made a suggestion too. 'Why don't you join our circus?' he said. 'You would make a fine beetle-tamer, dressed in that splendid gold suit. And the crowds would come from far and wide if they heard that General Marchmouse was in the ring!'

'Oh, yes, what a splendid idea!' cried Mr Mirth. 'You could be our star attraction!'

The General looked overwhelmed. It was such a thrilling proposal, his brain had started to spin.

'It's a fine life in the circus,' Mr Merry said temptingly. 'We'll give you your own wagon, with a dressing-table, and chocolate creams to eat!'

The General's heart quickened. He adored chocolate creams.

'And you get lots of money!' purred Mr Moody.

'And lots of fan mail!' Mr Mirth added silkily.

Suddenly all the mice were talking at once, egging him on. Their voices swam around him as if in a dream. The General closed his eyes, and saw it all . . . The crowds and the chocolates and the fan mail – and above all the open road, paved with adventure.

'Oh, yes!' he said. 'I'LL COME!'

Chapter Five

Nutmeg woke first the next day. She sat up in bed, and pulled her shawl around her. It was frosty and bright. The sun was shining through the broom cupboard window, and she could hear a bird rustling in the creeper.

She turned to Tumtum and gave him a shake. 'Wake up, dear!' she said. 'It's time to go and find the General!'

Tumtum groaned, and buried his head under the covers. He didn't like waking up.

Nutmeg left him in bed, and hurried downstairs. A little while later, Tumtum smelled sausages cooking.

Perhaps I will get up after all, he thought.

He got dressed, and went to find Nutmeg in the kitchen. They both had a big breakfast to keep their spirits up. After the sausages there was porridge and pancakes and a kedgeree, then a fruit salad with cherries on top. And they washed it down with hot milk and coffee.

'Well, we'd better be setting off,' Tumtum said, wiping the crumbs from his whiskers.

It was still early when they crept out into the kitchen of Rose Cottage, and no one had stirred.

The toy circus towered before them, with the big top flapping in the draught.

'If we find the General quickly, then we can have the bus back in place by the time the children come down for breakfast,' Nutmeg said. 'Just think how pleased they'll be to get it back!'

'Hmm, it should be possible,' Tumtum said. 'It's a Saturday, so the children will probably get up late. Come on, let's hurry up and find him. He can't have gone far in a small bus like that.'

They ran across the kitchen, and wriggled outside under the back door. Then they crossed the path, and clambered on to the lawn. They wished they had put on their waterproofs, for the grass came up to their waists, and it was sodden with dew.

They were in little doubt as to which way the General had gone. They trekked straight down to the farm gate at the bottom of the garden, and hurried into the meadow.

'Look how tall this gate is,' Nutmeg said, peering up at it. 'The bottom bar's so high up off the ground, there would have been plenty of room for the bus to go underneath.'

They walked on, but soon the grass became taller than their heads, and they couldn't see where they were going. It was like being in a forest.

'Oh, dear. We'll never be able to find the bus now!' Nutmeg said anxiously.

But then Tumtum saw a big rock poking out of the grass just ahead of them. 'Let's climb up there, then we'll be able to see where we are,' he said.

They traipsed over to it, and scrambled to the top. And when they stood up, they could see the whole meadow sloping away in front of them. Tumtum perched his field glasses on his nose, and carefully searched it all over.

'Can you see anything?' Nutmeg asked impatiently.

'There he is!' Tumtum cried finally. 'There's something red down by the stream! I can't see it clearly; it's too far away. But it must be him!'

He passed Nutmeg the field glasses, so she could have a look too. 'Yes, that must be the bus,' she said, seeing something red and shiny in the lens. 'But what's that big thing next to it? It looks like a balloon – or a huge tent. How very strange!'

Tumtum looked again, and now he saw it too.

Nutmeg was right, it did look like a tent. But it was too far off for him to be sure. 'How very odd,' he said. 'Come on, let's go and investigate.'

They scrambled down from the pebble, and started making their way through the grass. It was a long way, and it was nearly two hours before they reached the other side.

The grass round the stream was much shorter, and they could see all the way along the bank. And when they spotted Master Goldtail's big top, with Arthur's bus drawn up beside it, they stopped still in surprise.

'It must be a touring mouse circus!' Nutmeg said. 'But I didn't know there was a circus coming to the meadow. How strange that they didn't put up posters round the village!'

'Hmm. And it looks like the General's got mixed up with them somehow,' Tumtum said anxiously. 'Come on, we'd better go and see what's going on.'

They hurried towards the gate. And when they reached the ticket booth, they found a notice pinned to the window:

MASTER
GOLDTAIL'S
MOUSE CIRCUS
COME AND SEE
GENERAL
MARCHMOUSE
FIGHT A
GIANT BEETLE!!!!
1 p.m. Today

'He's joined the circus!' Nutmeg gasped.

'Well, he'll un-join it soon enough when I've spoken to him!' Tumtum said crossly. 'What nonsense! I'll soon talk some sense into him!'

He peered in the window of the ticket booth, but there was no one inside. So they walked in through the gate.

The circus seemed deserted; there was no one in sight, and not a sound coming from the wagons. And everything looked very tatty. Nutmeg was surprised. She had been taken to mouse circuses as a child, but they had all been spick and span – not a bit like this.

Something about the place made her feel uneasy.

'Let's look in those wagons over there, and

see if we can find who's in charge,' Tumtum said.

The wagons were lined up on the far side of the big top. They walked over to them nervously, wondering what they would find. The first wagon had a filthy woollen blanket hung across the bars.

'I say, is anyone at home?' Tumtum asked.

There was a sudden scrabbling noise. Then the corner of the blanket tweaked aside – and a big beetle glared out. When he saw Tumtum and Nutmeg he gave an angry hiss. He did not look at all pleased to be disturbed.

They hastily apologised, and tried the next wagon along. But this one was just full of cardboard boxes, sealed with brown tape and labelled 'FRAGILE'.

'I wonder what's in them,' Nutmeg

said curiously.

'Oh, probably just some circus tat,' Tumtum said. He wasn't interested in the boxes. He just wanted to find the General and go home.

The third wagon had a plush red curtain drawn across it, and a sign saying, 'DO NOT DISTURB.'

'Perhaps this is the ringmaster's wagon,' Tumtum said. 'It says not to disturb him, but I'm afraid we shall have to!'

Nutmeg watched anxiously as Tumtum stepped forwards, and called out through the curtain:

'I say, sorry to disturb you, but it's Mr and Mrs Nutmouse here, from Nutmouse Hall and — er, well . . . we just wondered if we could have a quick word with you, if you would be so kind. You see, we're looking for our friend . . .'

There was no reply, and they wondered if the wagon might be empty.

But then they heard someone yawn. It was a long, bored yawn. The sort of yawn that says, 'Oh, go away and leave me alone!'

And next moment the curtain swished aside, and General Marchmouse appeared!

The Nutmouses looked at him in astonishment. For this was not the General Marchmouse of yesterday, or the day before that. He had *completely* changed.

He was dressed in the gold suit that he had ripped from Arthur's doll, with a daisy in his button hole – and his whiskers had been dyed pink! He

68

suddenly looked most unGeneralish.

'Darlings, hello,' he purred, in a voice most unlike his usual one. 'Have you come to see the show?'

'Certainly not!' spluttered Tumtum, who found the General's new style most unsettling. 'What the devil are you playing at, General? How *dare* you steal Arthur's bus! You must drive us all back to Rose Cottage at once, and return it to the kitchen!'

'I'm afraid that is out of the question,' the General replied, peering down at them snootily. 'I have lent the bus to Master Goldtail, seeing as he has no transport of his own. And we shall need it this afternoon, when we drive off on the next stage of our tour!'

Tumtum and Nutmeg looked at him in horror. '*A TOUR!* Don't be so ridiculous!' Tumtum said. 'Just think what Mrs Marchmouse would say if she discovered you were touring with a circus! You are coming home with us!'

The General gave Tumtum a withering stare. His eyes had a dark glint. 'Oh, no I am not!' he said tauntingly. 'Can't you see, old boy, I'm a circus mouse now!'

Chapter Six

Tumtum and Nutmeg did all they could to make the General see sense.

'Just think what *The Mouse Times* will say when they learn that the Great General Marchmouse has joined a circus!' Tumtum cried. 'You'll be a laughing stock! The Royal Mouse Army will disown you!'

Tumtum felt sure this would bring the General to his senses – for he took great pride in

his army career. But the General didn't seem to care.

'It's no good, I'm not coming,' he said stubbornly. 'My army days are over. I've become a star of the circus, and I shall become the biggest star that ever there was! Now leave me alone. I've got to curl my whiskers for the show!'

And with that he stood up and swished shut the curtains.

Tumtum and Nutmeg were aghast.

'How *could* he be so beastly?' Nutmeg cried. 'Can you imagine what Mrs Marchmouse will say when we tell her he's run away to become a beetle-tamer! Oh, if only we hadn't invited him to supper at Nutmouse Hall, then none of this would have happened!'

'I've an idea,' Tumtum whispered. 'Let's drive the bus back to Rose Cottage ourselves! We've every right to take it – it belongs to Arthur, after all. And without a bus, the circus can't drive away. They'll be stuck here in the meadow until they find another means of transport. So in the meantime at least we shall know where the General is.'

'Oh, what a splendid idea!' Nutmeg said. 'We can let the General have his fun until Mrs Marchmouse comes home. Then *she* can come down here and talk some sense into him.'

Feeling very cheered by this plan, they slipped away from the General's wagon and crept over to the bus.

But when Tumtum tried the driver's door, it was locked. And the passenger door was

locked too.

'Blow!' he said.

'Let's see if the back door's open,' Nutmeg suggested – but then there was a sudden shout:

'OI! What are you doing?' a furious voice cried. 'Get away from that bus!'

They both jumped. And when they turned round they saw a clown marching towards them. It was Mr Merry. His fangs were bared, and he looked very frightening.

'I, er . . . We were just, er . . . just admiring it,' she said nervously.

'Well, now you've admired it you can push off,' the clown replied.

'That's no way to speak to –' Tumtum began, but Nutmeg gave him a sharp nudge. She sensed it

was time to go.

'Shh,' she whispered, 'don't get into a row.' She tugged Tumtum by the sleeve and they hurried out through the gate, while the clown stood glaring at them. 'Let's get away,' Nutmeg whispered. They walked on along the bank, until the circus was out of sight. Then they sat down on a pebble, feeling very shaken.

'Isn't it strange that a clown should be so horrid?' Nutmeg said. 'In fact, there's something strange about the whole circus. I didn't see any dragonflies or racing slugs, or the sort of things that a mouse circus usually has. There was just one tired old beetle. And their big top was in tatters, but the General's wagon had a smart chandelier. And did you notice those silver plates on his dressing table? I wonder where they got them from.'

'Hmm, it did seem odd,' Tumtum agreed. 'I'd like to go back and have another snoop. But I don't want to run into that clown again. I reckon we've already made him suspicious. There's no point asking him for the bus back – I shouldn't think he'd care one hoot if we told him it really belongs to Arthur!'

Nutmeg agreed. 'But we *must* get it back before this afternoon,' she said, 'or else the circus will drive away, taking the General with them! You can see that he's completely under their spell! And just think what a fool he's going to look if word of this gets out. His reputation as a famous war hero will be in tatters!'

The situation did look bleak. They both sat on the pebble, wondering what to do.

Then Tumtum had an idea. 'I know!' he said, jumping up excitedly. 'Let's go home, and write the children a letter, telling them that their bus has been stolen by another circus. We can explain exactly where it is — they know the stream very well. Then they can come down here this afternoon, and fetch it back!'

'Oh, what a smashing plan!' Nutmeg agreed.

But then she looked fussed. 'What about the General?' she said anxiously. 'I mean to say, if the children find him sitting there curling his whiskers in his wagon, they might take him prisoner!'

'Oh, I shouldn't worry,' Tumtum said. 'The children are so big, the General and the circus mice

will spot them a mile off, and they'll hide in the grass. And without a bus, the circus won't seem nearly so appealing to the General. He'll give up the whole adventure and head for home before anyone finds out about his silly jape!'

'Oh, I do hope so,' Nutmeg said.

There was no time to lose, so they hurried straight back across the meadow. But it took even longer this time, for they were going uphill. It was nearly midday by the time they reached the farm gate leading into the garden of Rose Cottage.

'At last!' Tumtum said, and at the sight of home his stomach gave a loud rumble. It seemed ages since breakfast, and he could hardly wait to tuck into a nice big lunch.

But as they were walking under the gate, a

field mouse appeared. The Nutmouses recognised him at once. It was little Timmy Twigmouse, whose father delivered the firewood to Nutmouse Hall. He appeared to be in a great hurry, and he looked very excited.

'Have you heard the news?' he asked breathlessly. 'There's a circus in the meadow, and would you believe it . . . *General Marchmouse has joined them!*'

Tumtum and Nutmeg gulped. News of the General's adventure had spread faster than they'd thought.

'When did you hear about this?' Tumtum asked anxiously.

'Oh, everyone's talking about it,' Timmy Twigmouse chirruped. 'The General's the star act.

He's going to FIGHT A GIANT BEETLE! Just think! It's going to be quite a show!'

'I say!' he said, noticing that they did not look very enthusiastic. 'You are going, aren't you?'

'Oh, I don't think we've time today,' Tumtum said vaguely, not wishing to let on what they knew. 'We'll go tomorrow.'

'But you can't go tomorrow!' Timmy Twigmouse cried. 'They won't be here tomorrow. Haven't you heard? This is a *ONE-OFF SHOW*! And when it's finished they're packing up and moving on to London. Their next performance will be in Covent Garden!'

Tumtum and Nutmeg looked at him in horror.

'London!' Nutmeg gasped. 'Are you sure?'

Timmy Twigmouse nodded. 'That's right,' he said. 'My father went round this morning to deliver them some firewood, and they told him all about it. They're going to drive all the way there in their new circus bus! This is the only chance to see them, so I'm going down there right now to make sure I get tickets!'

Timmy Twigmouse said goodbye, and hurried on his way. But Tumtum and Nutmeg stood by the gate, frozen with shock.

They had never been to London, but they had heard all sorts of alarming things about it. '*London!*' Nutmeg said faintly. 'But London's miles away! And it's full of bandit mice! Oh, Tumtum, we *must* stop him! Just think what kind of trouble he might get into there!'

Chapter Seven

After Tumtum and Nutmeg left, the General sat down at his dressing table, feeling a little deflated. Tumtum's words kept echoing round his head: 'Think what Mrs Marchmouse will say . . . Think what *The Mouse Times* will say . . . You will be in disgrace . . . disgrace . . . disgrace . . .'

The General pressed his paws over his ears,

trying to block the voice out. '*Bother Tumtum!*' he muttered. 'This is too good an adventure to miss. I'm not going to let him spoil my fun!'

He glanced in the mirror, thinking he would cheer up when he saw how handsome he looked. But even his reflection had lost its dazzle.

He stood up with a sigh, and took his whip from the bed. He was sure he would feel all right again once the show had begun.

'Tumtum is quite wrong, a beetle-tamer is a very fine thing to be!' he told himself firmly. 'When Mrs Marchmouse hears about it, she'll be proud of me! And she isn't due back from her sister's until Friday . . . our tour will probably have finished by then, and I shall be back home, so it's not as though she'll miss me!'

He felt a little cheered. And he decided to go and find Master Goldtail, to discuss his act. The show was due to start in less than two hours, but there had been no dress rehearsal.

But just as he was opening the door of his wagon, Mr Mirth appeared. He looked very agitated.

'Quick! Get in the bus, we're moving on!' he shouted.

'Moving on? But I don't understand,' the General said in astonishment. 'What about the show? The fans will be arriving soon.'

'Just do what I say – and buck up!' Mr Mirth snapped. Then he ran on down the line of wagons, slamming the doors, and fastening the tow ropes.

When the General stepped outside, he saw

that all the other mice were rushing about too. Mr Moody was pouring water on the campfire, and Mr Mirth and Master Goldtail were pulling down the big top!

The General could not understand it. 'What's happening?' he asked. But everyone was too frantic to explain.

In almost no time, the big top and the ticket booth had been loaded on to the wagons.

'Right, that's everything!' Master Goldtail shouted, leaping behind the wheel of the bus. 'Come on, everyone. Jump in, QUICK!'

The clowns all leapt on board. Only the General remained on the ground.

'*COME ON!*' Master Goldtail shouted, poking his head from the window. 'Hurry, or we'll

be caught!'

'*Caught?* Caught by whom?' the General asked – but then suddenly he heard a piercing whistle, so loud it made him jump.

Master Goldtail revved the engine, and the bus and the wagons lurched forwards through the grass. The General did not know where the whistle was coming from, or whose whistle it was. But he felt sure that something awful was going to happen.

'Wait for me!' he cried, tearing after them. Mr Mirth opened the back door and hauled him inside. Then off they sped along the bank, with the six wooden wagons clattering behind them.

Master Goldtail drove the bus as fast as it would go. *Bump, bump, bump* they went until they

reached the edge of the field; then they scraped through the hedge, and into the wood on the other side.

The clowns kept looking anxiously through the back windscreen, to see if they were being followed. The mood was very tense. No one said a word.

Deeper and deeper into the wood they drove, crunching through the bracken.

Eventually, when the trees had become so thick it was almost dark, Master Goldtail turned off the engine, and let out a deep sigh.

'Well, I reckon we've given them the slip all right,' he said. 'They'll never find us now.'

'We'll have to be more careful in future,' Mr Mirth said. 'I wonder how they found out about us?

I didn't think the word would spread so fast.'

'Found out *what?*' the General asked. 'Oh, *please* will someone tell me what's going on? Who were we running away from? Who was blowing that whistle so loudly?'

The others looked at him coldly.

'*Who?*' Master Goldtail sneered. 'Why, the policemice, of course! We can recognise their whistles a mile off. I don't know how many of them there were – there might only have been one, but there might have been half a dozen of them, running up on us through the grass. We weren't going to take any chances. If we'd hung around a minute longer, we'd have been arrested!'

'*Arrested?*' the General gasped. 'But why? What have we done?'

Mr Mirth gave a nasty cackle. 'Haven't you guessed what our game is, by now, General? We're not *real* circus mice. The ticket booth and the big top – they're just a cover-up. Our real job is BURGLING MOUSE-HOLES. That's what we do for a living!'

'Burgling m– *Good grief!*' the General stammered. He was too horrified to speak.

Mr Moody jerked a paw over his shoulder. 'In those wagons back there, we've got more gold and silver than you've ever set eyes on!' he said proudly. 'We're going to London, and we'll all be rich!'

'London?' the General gasped.

'That's right,' Master Goldtail said. 'It's a long way, but we reckon we'll get there in a month or two – especially now we've got this nice fast bus to drive. And there'll be lots of rich mouse-holes to burgle on the way!'

The General was appalled. He thought he had joined a circus – but instead he had fallen in with a gang of common thieves!

'I am leaving!' he said, flinging open his door. 'And when I see those policemice, I shall tell them which way you've gone!'

'Oh, but I wouldn't be so hasty, if I were you, General,' Master Goldtail said mockingly. 'You don't want to be caught by the police any more than we do!'

The General snorted. 'I'm not a thief!' he fumed. 'I've nothing to fear from the police!'

'Hah! What do you think the policemice will say when we tell them that you've stolen a bus?'

Master Goldtail snarled. 'You've supplied the getaway vehicle, General. You're as much a crook as we are! If the police catch us, you'll go to prison too.'

'What rot! I only borrowed the bus – I didn't steal it!' the General said furiously. 'Now let me out!'

He turned to the door, and made to lower himself to the ground.

'Get back in your seat,' Master Goldtail growled. His voice was ice cold – and when the General turned round, he saw that he had whipped out a gun.

'Close the door!' Master Goldtail barked, pointing the nozzle straight at the General's nose. 'This gun's loaded with sherbet.'

The General gulped, for as he knew very well, sherbet guns are horrid things. If a mouse is hit by one at close range, the sherbet burns his throat and stings his eyes, and turns his stomach into lemonade.

He squirmed back into his seat, and pulled shut the door.

Master Goldtail passed the gun to Mr Mirth, and started the engine. The bus gave a splutter, and lurched on through the wood.

The General was numb with fear. And it was not just the gun he was afraid of. The others were right — when the police found out he had taken Arthur's bus, they would think he was a thief too. He would be stripped of his medals, and sent to prison. Oh, the shame of it! The shame!

'Don't look so glum, General,' Master Goldtail sneered. 'You do as we say and we'll make sure you're all right. You can help us rob the village shop!'

'*The village shop?*' the General said feebly.

'That's right,' Mr Moody said. 'We're going to bust in after closing time, and gorge ourselves on cream cakes and jam tarts! And we'll steal all the tubes of sherbet to use in our guns!'

'And no one will catch us now we've got this speedy bus to escape in!' Mr Mirth gloated. 'We'll be able to carry out twice the number of robberies now! And it's all thanks to you, General!'

'Three cheers for General Marchmouse!' Mr Merry cried. 'Hip, hip, hooray! Hip, hip, hooray! Hip, hip, hooray!'

The General sat silently on the back seat, as if caught in a terrible dream. He thought of his wife, and of Tumtum and Nutmeg, and of all the army medals for which he had fought so bravely . . . but they seemed lost in a distant past.

Oh, if only he hadn't borrowed the wretched bus! But he had gone too far to turn back . . . he was a criminal now.

Chapter Eight

Meanwhile, back at Rose Cottage, Arthur and Lucy had been looking for the bus all morning.

They had searched the garden twice, and they had gone up and down the little lane that ran in front of Rose Cottage, peeking under the parked cars, and poking along the ditch.

But by lunchtime there was still no sign of it.

'Whoever stole it has probably driven out of the village by now,' Arthur said as they came back inside. 'I bet we'll *NEVER* get it back. And we'll never discover who the mysterious thief was either!'

They sat down to lunch feeling very glum. They did not say anything to their father about the missing bus, for they suspected he would not believe such a peculiar story. And this was their adventure – they didn't want any grown-ups interfering before they'd had a chance to solve it themselves.

Mr Mildew spent the whole meal with his head buried in a book, so it was easy to exclude him from the conversation.

'I think we should write to Nutmeg, and tell

her everything that's happened. I bet she'll know who took the bus, and perhaps she'll be able to help us find it,' Lucy said.

Arthur nodded. Lucy was right. This was just the sort of mystery Nutmeg might be able to solve. So as soon as lunch was finished they hurried upstairs to write her a letter.

But when they walked into the attic they got a big surprise – for Nutmeg had already been there. And she had left a letter for *them*! It was in the usual place, propped up against Lucy's hairbrush on top of the chest of drawers.

'Quick, let's see what it says,' Arthur said excitedly. 'Perhaps she knows about the bus already!'

Lucy grabbed the magnifying glass from her

bedside table, then she sat down on her bed, holding the letter in her palm.

'Oh, hurry!' Arthur cried impatiently. 'What does it say?'

Lucy was squinting. 'It looks like Nutmeg wrote it in a great hurry – her writing's even more squiggly than usual!' she said. Eventually, stumbling a little, she managed to read it out loud:

URGENT

Dear Arthur and Lucy,

Last night your toy bus was borrowed by a mischievous friend of mine. He only took it for a bit of fun, and I'm sure he intended to bring it back. But now the strangest thing has happened, for he has fallen in with a real

circus, which is camped down in the meadow.

And they plan to run away to London together,

travelling in YOUR BUS!

But you can stop them. You should go down to

the meadow at once, my dears, and snatch the

bus back! You will find it parked on the bank

of the stream, beside the willow tree. Now

hurry, for they plan to set off this afternoon!

Love,

Nutmeg.

The children were astonished.

'A friend of Nutmeg! But who could that be?' Arthur asked. 'And I wonder who the *real* circus belongs to.'

'Perhaps it's a fairy's circus!' Lucy said.

Arthur scrunched his nose. He did not believe in fairies, except for Nutmeg of course. And she was a Fairy of Sorts, which was different. 'Perhaps it's a Rats' Circus!' he said eagerly. 'Now *that* would be exciting!'

'Rats! Eugh! I hope not!' Lucy shuddered.

'Well whoever they are, we've got to stop them before they take my bus to London,' Arthur cried, leaping up from the bed.

The children set off at once. They tore down the garden, and clambered over the gate, wondering what they were going to find.

But the mystery was not going to be solved as soon as they hoped. For General Marchmouse's adventure had just taken a turn for the worse.

Chapter Nine

The children ran down the meadow until they were in sight of the stream. Then they stopped still, and stood peering along the bank. They could see the willow tree, but the ground around it was hidden by nettles.

They crept up to it on tiptoe, hoping to take the circus by surprise. But when they reached the tree, and searched all around it, the circus wasn't there.

'Nutmeg must have got the wrong tree,' Arthur said impatiently. 'Come on, we'll have to look all along the bank. It must be here somewhere!'

He ran back to the stream, and started poking about in the bushes. Lucy was about to follow him; but then she noticed something curious on the ground. To one side of the willow tree, there was a patch of grass that had been flattened, as though a bucket had been placed on it. And in the middle of it, she could see something glowing.

She wondered if it might be a bead, or a gold coin. But then she noticed little feathers of smoke rising from it. And when she knelt down and peered at it more closely she saw that it was a tiny campfire; and lying on the grass next to it was a frying pan the size of a penny.

'Arthur, quick, come and look at this!' she cried.

She held the pan in the palm of her hand, and they both studied it in astonishment.

'Yuck!' Arthur said. 'It's got a burnt fly in it!'

'And look at the fire!' Lucy said, pointing to the tiny pile of smouldering twigs. 'This must be where the circus was parked, you can see where the grass has been flattened by the wagons and the big top!'

'So Nutmeg was right, the circus *was* here!' Arthur cried. 'But we're too late. It's gone!'

'Well they won't have got far,' Lucy said. 'Their campfire's still burning, which means they can't have left long ago. But I wonder which way they went.'

Then Arthur noticed something else. 'Look here!' he said, pointing to two little tracks weaving through the grass. 'These must be the marks made by the wheels of the bus and the wagons.'

'Well spotted!' Lucy said. 'If we follow these, then we're sure to find them!'

They jumped up excitedly, and followed the trail along the grass by the bank of the stream. But when they reached the edge of the meadow, the ground turned to bare earth, and the tracks disappeared.

'Blow!' Arthur said. 'Now what do we do?'

'Well they can't have crossed the stream, there's no bridge,' Lucy said. 'They must have driven into the wood.'

'Then we'll never find them!' Arthur said glumly. 'The wood's huge, and it's full of bracken.'

'Yes, but if you go straight through it, you come out behind the church,' Lucy said. 'Well I bet that's what they've done. If they plan to drive all the way to London, they'll have to get on to a proper road at some stage. So they'll probably cut down through the church, and then on to one of the lanes leading out of the village.'

'All right then,' Arthur said. 'Let's see if we can find them on the road.'

They clambered over the stile at the bottom of the meadow, and followed the footpath along the edge of the wood until they reached the churchyard. Then they ran up the path to the gate, and let themselves out on to the lane.

To the right, the lane forked in two, with both ways weaving into the open countryside. To the left, it led past the war memorial and the village shop, then back towards Rose Cottage.

'Which way's London?' Arthur said.

'Let's go to the shop and ask Mrs Paterson,' Lucy suggested. 'She's sure to know.'

They hurried along, for it was nearly teatime, and the shop would be closing soon.

But just as they were crossing the lane towards it, Lucy suddenly stopped. 'Arthur, look!' she whispered. '*Over there!*'

She was pointing to the side of the shop, where the dustbins were kept.

'What is it?' Arthur asked.

'It was the bus!' Lucy said. 'I just saw it, really

I did – it went racing off behind those dustbins! And it was towing lots of wagons, but it was moving so fast I couldn't see very well.'

Arthur looked doubtful. He wondered why he hadn't seen it too. But they would know soon enough if Lucy had been imagining things: 'Come on, let's go and have a look,' he said. 'The alley's a dead end. If the bus did go down there, then we're sure to find it!'

They crossed the lane, and ran round to the side of the shop. The alley was very short, but it was full of old milk crates and cardboard boxes, so it took them a while to dig around. And just as Arthur was peering under a cardboard box, Mrs Paterson suddenly appeared. She had just closed the shop for the day, and now she was carrying out the rubbish. Her apron was covered in flour, and her make-up had smudged round her eyes. She looked very tired.

'Whatever are you doing here?' she asked the children in surprise.

'Er, I was . . . looking for something I'd lost,' Arthur mumbled. 'A . . . er . . . well, a toy bus actually!'

'Well, I'll let you know if I see it!' Mrs Paterson said. 'Now, hadn't you better be getting home? It will be dark soon. Your father will be worrying about you.'

'Yes, we're just going back now,' Arthur said, for he didn't want Mrs Paterson interfering in their secret search. 'And, er . . . one thing, Mrs Paterson. Do you know which way London is?'

'London? Well, it'll be about a hundred miles down there,' Mrs Paterson tutted, pointing up the lane towards the church. 'Why, are you planning to run away?'

'Oh, no . . . we were just, well . . . just wondering,' Lucy said hurriedly. 'Anyway, we'd better be getting home.'

The children said goodbye, then they turned and headed back towards Rose Cottage.

'Are you *sure* you saw it?' Arthur said.

'Quite sure! How many times do I have to tell you?' Lucy replied impatiently. 'It drove behind the bins, then it just sort of . . . vanished!'

'Well, if you're sure you saw it then we'll have to go back first thing in the morning and have another look,' Arthur said. 'It can't just have

116

disappeared. Perhaps it's hiding under one of those cardboard boxes, though I'm sure I looked under them all.'

'Yes, let's go back straight after breakfast,' Lucy said. 'Do you know, I feel *sure* we're going to find it!'

But the morning was still a long way off. There was the whole night to get through first, and all sorts of mysterious things were going to happen.

Chapter Ten

Tumtum and Nutmeg had spent an anxious afternoon in Nutmouse Hall, waiting for the children to come back from the meadow. But by teatime there was still no sound of them.

'They should have been home *ages* ago – it couldn't have taken them more than half an hour to run down to the stream and back,' Nutmeg said anxiously. 'Whatever can have happened?'

'Perhaps we had better go and look for them,' Tumtum said. But just as they were getting ready to go out, they heard a door slam, and then the thunder of feet in the kitchen.

'Oh, thank goodness! That must be them!' Nutmeg said.

They hurried out of their front gates, and crept to the edge of the dresser. The children had just come in from the garden, and when the Nutmouses saw that they had returned without the bus, they looked at each other in dismay.

'Whatever could have happened?' Nutmeg whispered. 'Why didn't they bring it back?'

She and Tumtum crouched beneath the dresser, trying to gather what had gone wrong.

'I wish it would hurry up and be the morning so we can go and have another look in that alley,' Arthur said.

'It's a good thing tomorrow's Sunday and there's no school,' Lucy said. 'Let's go and write Nutmeg a letter, telling her everything that's happened.'

'All right,' Arthur said. 'Just think how surprised she'll be when she learns that the circus has already gone!'

The children dashed upstairs, leaving Tumtum and Nutmeg in suspense.

'On the move already! Oh, how dreadful!' Nutmeg cried. 'But whatever could have happened? The children should have had plenty of time to snatch the bus before the circus set off!'

'Hmm. And I wonder what this alley is that they're referring to,' Tumtum said.

'They're sure to explain everything in their letter,' Nutmeg said. 'We shall just have to wait until we can read it.'

They did not dare follow the children up to the attic, for fear of being seen. So they waited impatiently under the dresser, until eventually Arthur and Lucy came downstairs. Lucy went into the larder, to find something for supper, and Arthur went to put his bicycle in the shed.

The mice seized their chance. They shot out from beneath the dresser, and dashed up the skirting board beside the stairs. Then they crossed the first floor landing, and slowly heaved themselves up the steep wooden steps to the attic.

When they finally crept into the children's bedroom, they saw a letter addressed to 'Nutmeg' propped against the mirror on the chest of drawers.

They climbed up to it, clutching on to the tights and socks which had been left tumbling from the drawers.

Then they anxiously unfolded it, and stood together at the bottom of the page, reading what it said:

Dear Nutmeg,

We went straight down to the meadow, just as you told us to, but the circus had gone! Then we thought we saw the bus on our way home, going down the alley at the side of the village

shop. We tried to follow it, but we couldn't

find it . . . and then Mrs Paterson appeared.

But we'll go and look again in the morning.

Love,

Arthur and Lucy.

'The morning might be too late!' Nutmeg cried. 'We shall have to go to the shop tonight, and try to persuade the General to come back! Oh, I do hope the circus is still there!'

'Let's go back to Nutmouse Hall and fetch our coats and a torch, then we can set out straight away!' Tumtum said.

They climbed back to the floor, and hurried downstairs. The children had moved into the drawing room, so they were able to dash back under the dresser unseen.

Then they ran into Nutmouse Hall and put on their warm clothes. But as they were about to leave the house, there was a sharp *Rap! Tap! Tap!* on the front door.

The Nutmouses looked at each other in surprise. They had not been expecting visitors tonight, and they wondered who it could be.

'Perhaps the General's come back!' Nutmeg said hopefully. But when Tumtum opened the door, they both got a big surprise.

It was Mrs Marchmouse. She looked very upset, and her nose was wet with tears.

'Mrs Marchmouse!' Nutmeg said in astonishment. 'We thought you were away looking after your sister – oh, goodness! Is she all right?'

But before Mrs Marchmouse could speak, a second mouse appeared.

This time, Tumtum and Nutmeg were even more taken aback. For it was Chief Constable Watchmouse, the head of the local Mouse Police Station! His snowy whiskers glared against his black uniform, and his big red nose was twitching.

He stood twisting his truncheon in his paws, looking very grave.

'Mr and Mrs Nutmouse,' he said, addressing them in his most solemn voice. 'I believe you might be able to assist me in my enquiries.'

'Assist you in . . . *Gracious me!* What's all this about?' Tumtum said, looking very alarmed.

The Chief Constable cleared his throat, clearly relishing the drama. But before he could explain his business, Mrs Marchmouse started sobbing out the story herself:

'Oh, Mr and Mrs Nutmouse, you will never guess what's happened!' she cried. 'I came home early from my sister's mouse-hole, seeing as she was so much better, and seeing as I was missing my poor Marchie so much . . . But when I let myself in, there was the Chief Constable, *searching the gun cupboard!* And he's got A WARRANT FOR MY HUSBAND'S ARREST!'

Tumtum and Nutmeg were astounded.

'*A warrant for his arrest?* Whatever do you mean?' Tumtum asked.

'They say he's joined a gang of thieves!' Mrs Marchmouse trembled. 'Oh, tell me it's not true, Mr Nutmouse! Tell me it's not true!'

'Gang of th–' Nutmeg stammered, hardly able to believe her ears.

'But, Chief Constable – there's been a terrible mistake!' Tumtum cried. 'The General hasn't joined a gang of thieves. He's joined a circus! We went to see him! Now, I can assure you, this is all a misunderstanding!'

But Mrs Marchmouse did not seem at all assured. At the mention of the circus, she started sobbing even harder.

The Chief Constable raised his truncheon, gesturing for calm.

'The information I have is that General Marchmouse has joined Master Goldtail's circus,' he said. 'Or should I say, Master Goldtail's circus that is *pretending* to be a circus . . . but that is not

129

really a circus at all!'

'*Not* a circus? But what do you mean, Chief Constable?' Tumtum asked, finding this all very confusing. 'They must be a circus – they've got wagons, and a big top!'

'Hah!' the Chief Constable snorted. 'You weren't the first to be fooled by all that, Mr Nutmouse! But I tell you, those wagons and that tent are just a front! Master Goldtail and his gang don't have one single drop of *real* circus blood in their tails!'

'But then who are they?' Nutmeg asked.

'They are *WANTED CRIMINALS*,' the Chief Constable announced dramatically. 'Burglars, Mrs Nutmouse – and very accomplished ones too. They have robbed more mouse-holes than you've eaten cockroach pies! Their wagons aren't used for carrying circus insects – they're used for carrying *stolen goods*!'

Nutmeg clapped her paw to her mouth in horror. No wonder the circus had given her such funny feelings! *They were thieves!* The cardboard boxes that she and Tumtum had seen stacked high in the second wagon must have been full of all the things they had stolen. And the silver in the General's wagon must have been stolen too! And to think that the poor General had been fooled by them!

'But why aren't they behind bars?' Tumtum asked.

'Because they are VERY CUNNING,' the Chief Constable replied. 'We call them the

131

Vanishing Circus: here one minute – and gone the next! I'll tell you how they operate, Mr Nutmouse. They turn up somewhere quite out of the blue – somewhere they've never been before, where the local mice don't know how wicked they are. Then they quickly knock up some posters, and put on a show. And very poor shows they are, from all I've heard – no trapeze, no dragonflies, just an old beetle! But the field mice all go, because it's not every day a mouse circus comes by – and, of course, they don't know how rotten the show's going to be until it's begun.'

'What about the clowns?' Tumtum interrupted.

'The clowns? Hah! That's the whole business!' the Chief Constable grunted. 'Only one of the clowns performs in each show. The other two sneak out while the field mice are in their seats and burgle their mouse-holes. And by the time everyone gets home and discovers they've been robbed, the circus has packed up and gone!'

'How shocking!' Nutmeg cried.

'But now the law's catching up with them,' the Chief Constable said confidently. 'The last set of burglaries they carried out were on Apple Farm, less than two miles away! So the police station down there sent me a telegram, warning me they might be coming this way!'

'Why haven't you been to arrest them?' Tumtum asked.

'Oh, believe me, I've tried!' the Chief Constable said. 'When I heard they'd arrived in the meadow, I rushed straight there. But they must have got wind I was coming, because by the time I reached their campsite, they'd gone! But I saw one of their posters tacked to a nettle stem. And imagine my surprise when I saw that General Marchmouse was topping the bill!'

'But it must be a mistake!' Mrs Marchmouse wept. 'Why would he want to get mixed up with wicked mice like that?'

Tumtum and Nutmeg agreed that there must have been a terrible misunderstanding.

'Now listen here, Chief Constable,' Tumtum said firmly. 'We spoke to the General this morning, and he had *no idea* that Master Goldtail was a crook. He thought the circus was real, just like we did. And he only joined it for a bit of fun. He'll change his mind soon enough when he finds out they're burglars! I wouldn't be surprised if he doesn't try to arrest them himself!'

But the Chief Constable did not look convinced. 'I have been reliably informed, Mr Nutmouse,' he said, 'that the circus is travelling in a stolen bus. And last night, towards the hour of seven o'clock, the General was seen driving that *very same* bus at considerable speed across the garden of Rose Cottage.'

The Chief Constable paused, to allow this dramatic information to sink in. 'I have three different field mice who will back up that version of events,' he added solemnly. 'So it would appear, Mr Nutmouse, that the General has not only teamed up with Master Goldtail and his gang . . .

he has supplied them with a getaway vehicle!'

Tumtum and Nutmeg looked horrified.

'But Chief Constable,' Tumtum said, 'this is quite unfair. It's true that the General took the bus last night – but he only meant to *borrow* it. He's borrowed the children's toys before, but he's always given them back! And he wouldn't have driven anywhere near that wicked circus-that-isn't-a-circus if he knew what sort of mice they were.'

The Chief Constable hesitated. He agreed that borrowing was not the same as stealing. Even so, the General had a lot to answer for. 'He must have found out by now that Master Goldtail and his mice are crooks – they've been on the run all afternoon,' he said. 'So why hasn't he come home?'

'They're probably holding him against his will,' Tumtum said. 'They'll be frightened that if they let him go he'll come and tell you where they are!'

'That's right!' Nutmeg cried. 'And I bet they think that when they reach London his famous name will attract more visitors to their shows!'

'Holding him against his will! Oh, how awful!' Mrs Marchmouse sobbed.

But the Chief Constable still had doubts. 'So long as the General is on the run, he remains under suspicion,' he said firmly. 'The important thing is to catch these rogues – *then* we can decide whether the General's guilty or not. But I've already searched the village high and low!'

'But *we* know which way they went!' Nutmeg

said. 'The children left us a letter just before you arrived, saying that they saw them disappearing down the alley beside the village shop!'

'The village shop!' the Chief Constable exclaimed. 'Well, well, I can guess why they've gone there. They'll be doing a break-in, I'll bet!'

Everyone gasped. 'But surely they're not planning to rob Mrs Paterson!' Nutmeg said in horror.

'Oh, yes! Believe me, Mrs Nutmouse, that is just the sort of mice they are!' the Chief Constable replied. 'They'll dig into her cream cakes, and steal all the gold coins from her till! COME ON!' he cried. 'Let's go and catch them red-handed!'

Chapter Eleven

The Chief Constable was longing to make an arrest. Master Goldtail was one of the most wanted mice in the country, so it was thrilling to think he might catch up with him at last. 'I shall set off at once!' he said gleefully, bounding from the door.

'But you'll never catch them on foot!' Tumtum cried. 'Not if they are in a bus. You must

take Arthur's police car!

'*A police car!*' the Chief Constable exclaimed. 'Does he have one? A *real* one, with a siren and an accelerator and a flashing light?'

'He certainly does,' Tumtum replied. 'It's parked just outside in the kitchen, behind the vegetable rack. I saw it there this afternoon. And it's a splendid car, I can tell you! Nutmeg and I had a test drive in it one night, and it went at a cracking pace!'

'That's right !' Nutmeg said excitedly. 'We'll come with you – there's plenty of room for us all to ride inside.' The Chief Constable's face glowed. He had always longed for a police car of his own, but the Mouse Police Force only provided cars for officers in the city.

'Are you sure the children won't mind us using it?' he asked anxiously.

'Of course not,' Tumtum replied. 'We'll leave them a note, explaining that we've borrowed it in order to arrest Master Goldtail, and rescue their bus.'

Everyone agreed that it was a capital plan.

'We must hurry,' Nutmeg said anxiously. 'Mr Mildew usually takes out the rubbish after supper. When he opens the back door, that will be our chance to drive the car outside!'

Nutmeg went to the drawing room, and hastily scribbled a letter to the children. Then she tucked it into her pocket, and they all hurried out of Nutmouse Hall.

The kitchen was deserted, but a light had

been left on, and when they peered across the floor they could just see the police car's yellow bonnet shining behind the vegetable rack.

They crept over to it. And when the Chief Constable saw the car he gave a whoop of joy. It was longer and sleeker than he could ever have dreamed, and it had a big blue siren and a walkie talkie!

He tugged open the driver's door, his heart thumping with glee. But then he suddenly jumped back in fear:

'Who's *that?*' he cried, pointing to the back seat.

Tumtum and Nutmeg laughed: 'Oh, that's nothing to be frightened of! It's only Arthur's toy policeman!' Nutmeg said.

'Goodness me!' the Chief Constable said, for it looked very fierce. It was sitting in the back seat, holding a pistol and a pair of handcuffs.

'He's a clockwork,' Tumtum explained. 'When you wind him up, he marches along, shouting, "Stop where you are, you are under arrest!" He makes Lucy's dolls tremble!'

'Let's take him with us,' the Chief Constable said eagerly. 'He'll frighten the wits out of Master Goldtail!'

'Where shall I leave the letter?' Nutmeg wondered. 'I haven't time to go and deliver it to the attic.'

'I've an idea,' Tumtum said. 'Why don't you leave it on Arthur's shoe. He always wears that pair on the doormat, so he'll find your letter when he puts them on in the morning.'

'Good idea,' Nutmeg said, and she ran over and tucked the letter into one of the laces.

Then they all jumped into the car. Tumtum sat in the front next to the Chief Constable, and Nutmeg and Mrs Marchmouse squeezed into the back, on either side of the toy policeman.

They waited silently. They didn't dare start the engine, for fear someone might hear.

Eventually, they felt the whole floor tremor, and when they peered up out of the windscreen they saw Mr Mildew striding in. They all sat still as stone, watching as he switched on the kettle, then started clattering some dishes in the sink.

Finally, he stooped down and heaved the bag out of the rubbish bin, then turned and pulled open

the back door.

'Get ready!' Tumtum whispered.

The Chief Constable flicked the key in the ignition, and the engine gave a gentle purr. They waited until Mr Mildew had walked some way down the path, towards where the bins were kept.

'Quick, go now!' Tumtum cried.

The Chief Constable pressed forward the gear stick, and the car glided across the kitchen floor, and slipped out of the doorway.

Mr Mildew was heaving the rubbish into the bin as the toy car slunk past behind him. The Chief Constable drove slowly, fearful of making too much noise. It was only when they had swung out on to the lane, that he dared to slam down his paw on the accelerator – then off they sped, with their

siren wailing.

The village was dark and still. The fires had been lit, and the televisions were flickering behind the curtains. No one saw the little toy car racing towards the village shop.

Nutmeg and Mrs Marchmouse clung to their seats, for the Chief Constable was driving at a terrifying speed. When they reached the shop he screeched to a halt. The shutters had been pulled down, and there was a 'Closed' sign hanging from the door. But there was light coming from the windows of Mrs Paterson's flat, on the floor above.

'Try down the alley,' Tumtum said. 'That's where the children thought they saw them.'

The Chief Constable sped round the side of

the building. They came into a forest of crates and dustbins, towering ghoulishly in the moonlight.

They raced round them, skidding and looping. Round and round they went, searching behind every box and bin. But the circus bus wasn't there.

The Chief Constable thumped the steering wheel in frustration. 'We're too late!' he said furiously. 'The scoundrels have gone!'

'They must have left for London already!' Mrs Marchmouse sobbed. 'Now I'll never get my husband back!'

Everyone felt wretched. But then Tumtum noticed something in the headlights. 'Hey, look over there!' he said, pointing ahead. 'That's where they must have broken in!'

They all peered through the windscreen. The

Chief Constable had stopped the car at the bottom of the alley, beside a tall thin door leading into the back of the shop. The door was made of glass, and the bottom pane had been broken. The hole was just big enough for a mouse to get through.

'Hah! So they *did* break in, as I suspected!' the Chief Constable said. 'I shall go inside and take some paw prints.'

He grabbed his truncheon, then he turned to Tumtum, and flung him a pair of handcuffs. 'Come on, Mr Nutmouse!' he said. 'Let's see if they're still in there.'

Tumtum clambered nervously out of the car.

'Don't forget the toy policeman!' Nutmeg said, for she was frightened Master Goldtail and his gang might become aggressive.

Nutmeg and Mrs Marchmouse jumped out, and helped Tumtum drag the policeman from the back seat.

They turned him round, so that he was facing the door of the shop, then Tumtum took hold of the silver dial on his back, and wrenched it in three full circles.

The policeman shuffled his feet, and his eyes rolled in their sockets. 'Stick 'em up!' he cried. 'You are under arrest!'

Then the policeman marched forwards, and smashed through the broken pane of glass. Tumtum and the Chief Constable scrambled after him, while Nutmeg and Mrs Marchmouse waited anxiously outside.

It was very black inside the shop. All they

could see was the outline of a pile of flan cases, towering in front of them. They crept round it, with the policeman marching alongside. Then they took out their torches, and shone them round.

They both gasped, for the shop was in a terrible mess. On every shelf, packets of crisps and biscuits and jam tarts had been gnawed open; and sweet wrappers nibbled to shreds.

'Come out, wherever you are!' the Chief Constable shouted. 'Do you hear me? This is the police! Come out, with your paws above your heads!'

'Stick 'em up! Stick 'em up!' the toy policeman squeaked.

There was not a sound.

'Blast, they've gone!' the Chief Constable

muttered. 'But what's happened to the General? He would *never* have assisted in a burglary like this. They must be holding him against –'

But then the Chief Constable shone his torch on to the cake shelf, and gave his whistle a piercing shrill. And when Tumtum span round, he saw the most astonishing sight:

It was General Marchmouse, trapped in a chocolate éclair! What a sight he looked. He was sunk in it up to his waist, and it was so sticky he couldn't get out. His gold suit was covered in goo and he looked very embarrassed.

'Come down with your paws above your head! You are under arrest!' the Chief Constable shouted.

'I can't come down. Can't you see I'm stuck?!'

the General replied, blushing furiously. 'Now get me out of here. This burglary was nothing to do with me. All I did was borrow a silly old bus.'

Hearing the commotion, Nutmeg and Mrs Marchmouse came running in from outside. When she saw her husband, Mrs Marchmouse let out a cry of relief – but she could see there was a lot of explaining to be done.

'Get me down! My boots are sodden!' the General cried.

The Chief Constable stared at him coldly. The evidence looked very damning. But Tumtum still could not believe that the General had been part of the robbery. 'Let's get him down, and hear what he has to say,' he said.

He and the Chief Constable climbed up to

the shelf, and between the two of them they pulled General Marchmouse out of the éclair, and helped him down to the floor.

'All right then, General,' the Chief Constable said gruffly. 'What's been going on here?'

'Oh, Constable!' the General spluttered. 'I have been most hideously abused! Master Goldtail and his gang forced me to come in here and help them load up their wagons with stolen sherbet. And they said that if I didn't do as I was told they'd throw me in the liquorice jar, and leave me there for Mrs Paterson to find in the morning!

'But I escaped by bravely burrowing inside a chocolate sponge cake. They hunted high and low for me, but I was too well hidden. You should have heard them cursing! Anyway, I waited until they'd

left, then I crawled out, and I was going to come straight to the station to tell you what had happened. But I didn't have a torch, and next thing I stepped into an éclair! And now everyone will think I'm a criminal, just because I borrowed Arthur's bus . . . but I only borrowed it for a bit of fun! And it was my birthday, after all.'

Tumtum and Nutmeg and Mrs Marchmouse could tell at once that the General was telling the truth. He had been very wrong to take Arthur's bus. But it was clear that he had been horribly fooled by Master Goldtail and his gang. They looked anxiously at the Chief Constable, wondering if he would be persuaded too.

The Chief Constable was scratching his chin.

'You have been a very foolish mouse,

General,' he said eventually. 'And next time you borrow a toy bus without permission I might not be so lenient! But for now you have been punished enough.'

Tumtum and Nutmeg and Mrs Marchmouse looked very relieved. 'Oh, thank goodness!' Mrs Marchmouse cried.

The General was relieved too, for he had feared he might go to prison. But he was too proud to let his gratitude show.

'Well, I'm glad that's cleared up then,' he said briskly. 'Now I can go home and have a hot bath.'

'Not so fast, General,' the Chief Constable said. 'We need to catch this gang, and FAST. Have you any idea where they went?'

'Well, yes. Now you come to mention it, I

think I do,' the General replied.

'*Where?*' the Chief Constable asked excitedly.

Everyone looked at the General, waiting to hear what he would say. There was an atmosphere of great suspense. The General knew his news would come as a big surprise, and he started to feel rather important.

He brushed a blob of cream off his jacket, trying to look more as a General should.

'I regret to inform you,' he announced dramatically, 'but Master Goldtail and his gang have GONE TO BURGLE NUTMOUSE HALL!'

Chapter Twelve

E veryone gasped.

'They've gone to burgle Nutmouse Hall!' Nutmeg cried. 'Oh my, oh my! They'll take our family portraits and our silver candlesticks and our crystal glasses and our gold goblets and our stuffed ladybirds and our rare books and . . . and . . .'

She clapped a paw to her mouth, too upset to

continue. Tumtum was distraught too.

'Have they gone straight there?' he asked anxiously.

'No, the robbery's planned for tomorrow evening,' the General replied. 'They've got to do some repair work first on their wagons.'

'Where are they tonight?' the Chief Constable asked.

'I couldn't really gather,' the General replied. 'Master Goldtail just said, "OK, let's camp under the rhubarb again!" and the clowns all agreed with him. Well, I didn't want to ask which rhubarb he meant, for fear of making him suspicious. Master Goldtail doesn't like being asked questions, you know.'

'*The rhubarb*,' the Chief Constable said

thoughtfully. 'Hmm, that could be anywhere. The village is full of rhubarb – just about every garden has got some. We could search all night, and still not find them. We shall have to wait until tomorrow, and catch them when they go to Nutmouse Hall.'

Everyone agreed that it was pointless looking for the thieves now. 'You must all spend the night with us,' Nutmeg said firmly. 'We've plenty of food, and we can all drive home together in Arthur's car.'

'An excellent plan,' the Chief Constable said. He lived alone, and he would be glad of some company after such an eventful day. The General was pleased too, for he didn't want to walk home alone knowing that Master Goldtail and his gang were still lurking in the village.

Nutmeg was glad to have guests to fuss over. It would take her mind off all the worrying things that had been taking place. 'Now, let's see,' she said. 'I shall put the General and Mrs Marchmouse in the green bedroom . . . and the Chief Constable can have the blue bedroom, next to ours and . . .',

THUD!

Everyone froze.

THUD!

It was footsteps on the stairs! Then suddenly the door behind the shop counter burst open, and on went the lights!

'It's Mrs Paterson,' Tumtum cried. '*RUN!*'

They all fled to the door, and scrambled out through the broken pane of glass. They could hear Mrs Paterson shrieking behind them: 'Help! Help!

I've been robbed!'

'Quick! Get into the car!' the Chief Constable shouted. They all jumped in, the General squeezing between Nutmeg and Mrs Marchmouse in the back. Then the Chief Constable revved the engine and off they sped, tearing back towards Rose Cottage.

The passengers all peered anxiously through the back windscreen, frightened Mrs Paterson might come running after them.

'Do you think she saw us?' Nutmeg asked.

'I don't think so,' Tumtum said. 'We were very quick – we got out before she came in. And if she had seen us, she'd have come chasing after us by now.'

'Doesn't this feel strange!' Mrs Marchmouse

said nervously. 'Here we are, running away as though *we* were the criminals!'

'Hmm, isn't it a pity humans can't hear what mice say,' Tumtum said. 'Otherwise we could have told Mrs Paterson the whole story.'

As it was they all felt very glad they had got away. For if Mrs Paterson had seen them she would have suspected they had made all the mess – and they dreaded to think what she would have done if she caught them.

The Chief Constable did not stop until he reached Rose Cottage. Then he parked beside the garden door, and they crept back inside.

It was late now, and the Mildews had all gone up to bed. The kitchen was very dark. Tumtum led them across the floor with his torch, and let them

into Nutmouse Hall.

They were all very shaken. But they felt better when they had had something to eat. Nutmeg warmed up the cockroach pie she had made for the General's birthday feast, and everyone tucked in hungrily. They washed it down with a strong pot of tea. Nutmeg did not offer them the birthday cake or the trifle or the jellied flies – for the mood was not festive enough for such party food.

Everyone was very worried about tomorrow. The General was the only one who felt talkative, and the others were too tired to stop him.

'So there we were, speeding off through the bracken yesterday afternoon – and I had no idea what was going on!' he recalled. 'Then the scoundrels came clean, and told me they were thieves! Well, you should have seen the fuss I made! "Stop the bus!" I cried. "I am going to get out and report you to the police!" But blow me if they didn't tie me up and gag me . . . but I struggled as bravely as I could . . .'

On and on he boasted, though his memory was a little flawed. '. . . So imagine my relief when you finally arrived in the village shop,' he said finally. 'Though I can tell you, I got quite a fright when I saw that toy police–'

'*Oh, no!*' Nutmeg cried, dropping her fork with a clang. 'The toy policeman! *WE FORGOT HIM!*'

Everyone groaned. It was true. In their haste to escape, they had left the policeman behind

in the shop.

'Oh, well, there's nothing we can do about it now,' the Chief Constable said. 'And the shop's in such a mess. I'll bet Mrs Paterson doesn't even notice the policeman tonight. I'll drive over there first thing in the morning, and see if I can sneak in and get him back.'

'All right,' Tumtum said, feeling a little reassured. 'Well, I suggest we get some sleep. We've a big day tomorrow, we shall need to be alert.'

Everyone agreed, for they were very tired. Even the General was flagging. His eyes had become heavy, and he suddenly hadn't the strength to go on boasting.

Tumtum bolted the front door, and locked all

the windows. Then Nutmeg showed the guests to their rooms, and they were asleep almost as soon as they had pulled up the covers.

Tumtum fell straight asleep too. But Nutmeg lay awake worrying. How she wished they hadn't left the toy policeman behind. Somehow she felt sure it would lead to trouble. And next morning her fears were confirmed.

For as the mice breakfasted in Nutmouse Hall, they heard the Mildews' door bell ringing, so loud it made them jump.

'I wonder who it could be, calling so early on a Sunday morning,' Nutmeg said.

They stopped eating, and sat with their ears pricked. They heard Mr Mildew's footsteps coming down the cottage stairs, then a worried voice sounding from the hall.

Nutmeg recognised it at once: 'It's Mrs Paterson!' she said in alarm.

They tried to hear what she was saying. But then Mr Mildew started talking at the same time, and the conversation became very difficult to follow.

Tumtum and Nutmeg left their guests at the table and crept out under the dresser to try and discover what was going on.

And when they peeked into the kitchen they saw Mrs Paterson standing by the table, clearly very upset. She had a duffel coat pulled over her dressing gown, and her face was drained of colour. In her hand was the toy policeman.

'I was burgled in the night, Mr Mildew.

Burgled!' she cried. 'Oh, you should see the mess! They gobbled my cupcakes, and burst open the cornflakes! And they stole *all the sherbet*!'

Arthur and Lucy were standing by the kitchen table, looking very uncomfortable.

'Yes, Mrs Paterson, I understand that, and I am very sorry,' interrupted Mr Mildew. He was wearing his dressing gown too, and looked a little bleary. 'But I still don't quite see what you think we've got to do with it.'

'I told you!' Mrs Paterson cried, waving the toy policeman. 'I found *this* lying on the floor, right next to my flan cases! And look, it's got Arthur's name scratched on it!' She turned the toy round, pointing to where the letters A. MILDEW had been scratched out with the tip of a compass on

the policeman's plastic back. 'Your children must have crept in, and dropped this while they were pinching my sweets! They'd have had plenty of opportunity – I didn't lock the back door until after nine.'

'But, we didn't!' Arthur cried.

'Then how do you explain this?' Mrs Paterson said, turning to wave the toy policeman at him. 'And what were you doing snooping round my dustbins yesterday afternoon?'

'Well, do you know anything about this?' Mr Mildew asked the children. Nutmeg thought his tone was rather sharp.

Arthur and Lucy looked very awkward. They had found Nutmeg's letter earlier that morning, so they knew it was her who had taken their police

173

car to the village shop.

But they didn't know what had happened next. Lucy tried to explain everything – or at least as much as they knew – even though she felt sure the grown-ups wouldn't believe her.

'On Friday night, Arthur's bus disappeared, and we looked everywhere, all over the garden, and all round the house, but we couldn't find it,' she began. 'Then yesterday afternoon, we thought we saw it driving down the little alley beside the shop . . . and when we told our friend Nutmeg about it, she said she had discovered that the bus had been stolen by a gang of thieves, led by a wicked villain called Master Goldtail . . . so she borrowed our toy police car and the policeman to go and arrest them, before they could do any more harm . . . but the bus hasn't come back, and the toy policeman got left behind in your shop . . . so Nutmeg's whole mission must have gone wrong!'

'Oh, what poppycock!' Mrs Paterson cried. 'They're making fun of me!'

The children looked at their father anxiously. Surely *he* would believe them? But Mr Mildew clearly thought it was ridiculous too.

'This is no time for silly stories, you can see that Mrs Paterson is upset,' he said.

'But it's not a silly story. It's what happened! *It is!*' Arthur cried.

'That's enough,' Mr Mildew said sharply. 'I want you both to go up to your room. And you can stay there until you're ready to discuss this sensibly – and tell me how the toy policeman really ended up in Mrs Paterson's shop.'

'Oh, Tumtum, what a terrible mess!' Nutmeg whispered. 'The children are in disgrace and it's all our fault!'

'Come on,' Tumtum said, 'let's hurry back to Nutmouse Hall and tell the others what's happened. We *must* catch Master Goldtail tonight, otherwise the children will never clear their names!'

The mice hurried back into the broom cupboard. As they let themselves through the front gates, they heard Arthur and Lucy trudging upstairs.

The children felt miserable. It was horrid of their father to take Mrs Paterson's side.

'Whatever could have happened?' Arthur said, flinging himself down on his bed. 'I wonder

176

why Nutmeg left the toy policeman behind.'

'Well she's bought the police car back,' Lucy said. 'I saw it outside on the doorstep. So at least Nutmeg must have got home safely. But I suppose Master Goldtail must have got away in the bus.'

'Well, unless Nutmeg catches him, Mrs Paterson will *never* believe our story,' Arthur said wretchedly. 'Oh, dear. Now *everything's* gone wrong!'

Chapter Thirteen

Tumtum and Nutmeg hurried back to Nutmouse Hall to tell the others what had happened.

'Don't you worry, Mrs Nutmouse,' the Chief Constable said confidently. 'I'll catch Master Goldtail and his good-for-nothing gang, and then the truth will come out!'

He took a pair of handcuffs from his kit bag,

and started polishing them with his napkin. It was several weeks since he had last made an arrest, and he was very excited.

'I'll teach them what happens to mice who break into village shops!' he said fiercely. 'I'll catch them red-handed when they turn up tonight!'

He checked his watch impatiently, wishing the evening would come.

But the General looked grumpy. He wanted to be in charge.

'This is *my* adventure,' he thought. 'And that silly old policemouse has NO RIGHT to tell me what to do! *I* gave him the tip-off that Master Goldtail and his gang were coming to burgle Nutmouse Hall, so *I* should be allowed to arrest them all by myself!'

The General knew that the arrest of Master Goldtail would be reported in *The Mouse Times*, and he couldn't bear to think that the Chief Constable would get all the credit for it. 'It should be *my* victory!' he thought.

Then suddenly he remembered something very important.

'You had better leave this arrest to me, Chief Constable,' he said grandly. 'It will need a General's expertise!'

The Chief Constable looked at him in astonishment. 'Leave it to *you*? But you're not a policemouse!' he said indignantly. 'This is my job!'

The General smiled smugly. 'The problem is, I don't think you can handle this yourself,' he said, 'seeing as Master Goldtail and his gang have sherbet guns –'

'*SHERBET GUNS?*' the Chief Constable spluttered. 'Are you sure?'

The General nodded: 'They've got one each. They stocked up on powder when they broke into the village shop.'

There was a stunned silence. They all knew how dangerous sherbet guns were.

'Oh, help us! What shall we do?' Mrs Marchmouse cried.

'There is no need to fear,' the General said bossily. 'The Royal Mouse Army trained all its officers to deal with sherbet attacks. We shall be quite all right, so long as everyone does exactly what I say.'

The Chief Constable looked furious. He

182

could see that the General was trying to take command. 'You are not telling me what to do!' he snapped.

'Oh, don't let's bicker,' Nutmeg said. 'We must protect ourselves. Chief Constable, do you have any other policemice who might help us?'

The Chief Constable shook his head. 'We're under-staffed just now,' he said. 'My DCI's away on holiday, and my sergeant's off with flu. We could summon reinforcements from the police station in town – they've got a dozen officers on duty. But it would take them two days to get here.'

'And what about the Royal Mouse Army?' Tumtum asked.

'No good. The troops are down on Apple Farm, seeing off some rats from the hay barn,' the

General replied briskly. 'We'd never be able to fetch them back in time.'

'Well then,' Tumtum said anxiously. 'It looks as if we're on our own.'

'Indeed we are, but we can still win!' the General said with relish. 'We must march up to the attic, and borrow ammunition from Arthur's toy soldiers – guns, grenades, swords, all the weapons we can carry.'

'All right, I'm sure Arthur won't mind,' Tumtum said. 'But there's to be no marching in Rose Cottage – when we go up to the attic, we shall have to sneak.'

The General nodded. 'And we shall need a toy tank too,' he said. 'Have the children got one?'

'Yes!' Nutmeg cried. 'There's one in the

184

drawing room. It's been there for weeks, tucked behind the sofa. I think Arthur must have forgotten about it.'

'Good,' the Chief Constable said, trying to take control. 'General, Tumtum – you can come with me after dark, and drive it back to the kitchen. We can park behind the laundry basket, or somewhere the children won't see us. Then we'll take Master Goldtail and his gang by surprise as they sneak in under the garden door! Just think what a fright they'll get when they see an army tank trundling towards them!'

The Chief Constable was thrilled. Guns and tanks sounded much more fun than a truncheon.

'I'll drive!' the General said grandly. And the Chief Constable was too excited to argue.

So the plan was agreed, and the rest of the day was spent preparing for the attack. They intended to catch the thieves before they reached Nutmouse Hall, but even so, they didn't take any chances. Tumtum and the Chief Constable went all round the house, boarding up the doors and windows, and the General set tripwires in the drawing room and the butler's pantry. Nutmeg and Mrs Marchmouse stuffed the chimneys with bedclothes and tapestries, in case they tried to bomb sherbet from the roof.

Lunch was a hasty affair, for they were all too nervous to eat much. As soon as the plates had been cleared, Tumtum and the General and the Chief Constable crept out into the kitchen and up to the attic to raid the toy barracks. They reappeared an

hour later with toy guns and grenades thrust in their belts.

'Goodness, you do look fierce!' Mrs Marchmouse said.

'Did you see the children?' Nutmeg asked anxiously.

'Yes, they are in the drawing room,' Tumtum said. 'So we shan't be able to collect the tank yet – they'd be sure to see us. We shall have to wait until they go upstairs.'

'And what about Mr Mildew?' she asked.

'Oh, he's all right,' Tumtum said. 'He's shut away in his study. We could hear his typewriter keys clanking.'

Nutmeg made a pot of tea, and they sat anxiously in the kitchen. Tumtum and the Chief

Constable took turns to creep out of the broom cupboard, to see if it was safe to go into the drawing room. But the children were milling about all afternoon.

Then Mr Mildew came into the kitchen to make supper; and it wasn't until nearly eight o'clock that the Chief Constable was able to report that everyone had gone upstairs.

'Come on, we must hurry up and get the tank!' the General said. 'Master Goldtail might arrive at any minute!'

Tumtum and the General leapt up, and followed him to the door.

'Oh, do be careful!' Nutmeg cried.

The mice crept out into the Mildews' kitchen. It was very dark. The lights were out, and they could see stars shining at the window.

Tumtum pulled out his torch, and they set off towards the drawing room. But when they were halfway across the kitchen they heard a sudden roar. And next moment there was a screech of brakes. The noise was coming from outside. And when they span round, they saw lights flashing under the back door!

'*It's them!*' the General hissed. 'Quick, hide!'

The mice darted behind a pile of telephone directories. And when they peeked out they saw four torches being shone round the floor.

'Keep back! Don't let them see us!' Tumtum hissed.

'Ha, Ha!' cried a nasty voice. 'Let's go and blast Mr Nutmouse with sherbet and steal all his

190

valuables! We'll take his chandeliers and his silver candlesticks and his gold tapestries and his fancy soup tureens! Ha! Ha! We'll be as rich as can be!'

'That's Goldtail!' the General said grimly.

'Fetch the tank!' Tumtum whispered. 'And HURRY!'

Chapter Fourteen

Master Goldtail and his gang had never been to Rose Cottage before. They flashed their torches round the kitchen, searching for the gates to Nutmouse Hall.

'Where the devil are they?' Master Goldtail snarled. He grabbed a piece of paper from his pocket, and read out the address again:

Nutmouse Hall
The Broom Cupboard
The Kitchen
Rose Cottage

'Well, this is the kitchen. But I can't see a broom cupboard!'

'It must be here somewhere,' said Mr Moody. 'Nutmouse Hall is the most famous mouse house in the whole county.'

'We've got to find it. I'm not leaving here empty-handed!' said Mr Merry.

They hunted on, flashing their torches round the skirting board.

Meanwhile, Tumtum and the others crept out from behind the telephone directories, and tiptoed

into the drawing room.

Tumtum was glad that Nutmouse Hall was so well hidden. But he knew the thieves would find it in the end.

'We must hurry,' he whispered. 'Imagine how frightened Nutmeg and Mrs Marchmouse will be if they break in!'

One of the drawing-room lamps had been left on, and they could just see the tank peeking out from behind the sofa.

They raced over to it. And when the General saw it close up his eyes glinted. He had driven tanks in the Royal Mouse Army, but never one like this. It was as big as a cake tin, and its gun was the size of a rattle!

Tumtum and the Chief Constable had never

operated a tank before, but the General reckoned he knew just what to do. He scrambled up the ladder, and wrenched open the hatch. 'Quick! Get in!' he shouted. Tumtum and the Chief Constable heaved themselves up after him, then they all slid into the tank.

Tumtum pulled the hatch shut, and everything went black. The General fumbled his way to the driver's seat, and started blindly running his paws across the controls. There were dozens of buttons and switches. He groped about, pulling this one and that, until eventually a pale green light came on.

They all looked about them in surprise. They were in a small, grey cabin, and every wall was covered with switches, saying things like 'FIRE!'

and 'FULL SPEED!' Everything was mouse-sized.

'Come on, General – let's go!' Tumtum cried, fearing Nutmeg and Mrs Marchmouse might be in danger.

The General slammed some more knobs on his dashboard, but he could not get the tank to start.

'Drat!' he said.

Then he saw a big red button labelled 'GO!' He gave it a push – finally the engine shuddered to life, and the tank ground forwards across the carpet.

Vroom!

Grrrrrrr!

Crrrrrrrrr-unch!

The tank's huge rubber tracks bulldozed

196

across a game of Snakes and Ladders, and over a discarded crisp wrapper.

Tumtum and the Chief Constable crouched behind the General, peering through the bulletproof windscreen.

'Straight ahead, left around the coffee-table leg, then hard right into the hall!' Tumtum said.

The General drove faster and faster, until finally they clattered into the kitchen.

'There they are!' the Chief Constable cried.

Master Goldtail and his mice were standing at the edge of the dresser, staring at the tank in astonishment.

'By Jove!' Tumtum said. 'We got here just in time.'

'Let's get them!' the General cried. The Chief

Constable heaved round the rotating gun, until it was pointing towards the dresser.

They could see the thieves in the headlights, frantically loading their sherbet guns.

'Hah! They can't harm us with their silly old sherbet!' the General snorted. 'We're in a sealed tank!'

But he spoke too soon. For at that moment the Chief Constable – who was quite senseless with excitement – leapt up, and pushed open the hatch.

'Stop! What the devil are you doing?' Tumtum cried. He tried to pull him back, but the Chief Constable was too fast. And before Tumtum could stop him, he poked out his head through the hatch, and shrilled his whistle.

'Hands up! YOU ARE UNDER ARREST!'

he cried.

'Get back, you fool!' the General shouted. But it was too late. For suddenly there was a deafening volley of gunfire, and a great blizzard of sherbet tore into the air. There was sherbet everywhere, swirling all around them. Soon the whole windscreen was smothered.

The Chief Constable stumbled back inside the tank, gasping for air. He was covered with yellow powder from his ears to his chin, and his throat was burning.

The General leapt up, and yanked down the hatch. But before he could shut it properly, a cloud of sherbet floated down into the tank, turning the air a thick, dusty yellow. The General had his handkerchief clapped to his mouth. But Tumtum

was taken unawares, and started coughing violently.

'W . . . W . . . Water!' he spluttered, collapsing beside the Chief Constable on the floor.

The General looked at them in horror. Tumtum's face had turned purple, and the Chief Constable was bright green.

The General knew that if he did not find them water they would choke. He staggered about the tank, yanking the controls. 'Water, water! A tank *must* have water!' he cried. But there was not a drop to be found.

Then, through the haze of sherbet, he saw a lever on the wall, with a sign saying:

PULL ONLY IN THE EVENT OF AN EXTREME EMERGENCY.

'This is an extreme emergency,' he decided. And he grabbed it with both paws and wrenched it down.

Then something wonderful happened.

Three green sprinklers dropped down from the ceiling, and fierce jets of water whooshed out, washing all the sherbet away.

Tumtum and the Chief Constable struggled to their knees, raising their faces to the cool spray. The water stopped their coughing, but it was some moments before they could speak.

'Gracious! I thought we were done for!' Tumtum said weakly.

'Pah! I've survived far worse attacks in my Royal Mouse Army days,' the General boasted. 'Why, you should have seen the Battle of the –'

But he was cut short by another deafening rattle of gunfire, and then the next round of sherbet smacked against the tank.

'I'll show them not to fire their sherbet guns at me!' the General fumed. He flung himself back into the driver's seat, and flicked on the windscreen wipers. Then he rammed his paw on the accelerator. The tank surged forwards, clattering across the tiled floor.

The General could see Master Goldtail and his accomplices in the headlights, and he drove straight at them.

The thieves hastily reloaded their guns, hoping to force the tank back with another blast of sherbet.

But while they were fumbling with their

ammunition, the General swung round the tank's machine gun until it was pointing straight at them, and thumped down his paw on a big red button marked 'FIRE!'

All at once, a ferocious jet of water tore out of the nozzle of the gun, and swept the thieves off their feet, rolling them across the floor like tennis balls.

'Ha, ha! That'll teach you to fire sherbet at us!' the General cried, crashing the tank towards them.

The thieves squealed in terror. There was water blasting all around them, and they could see the hazy outline of the toy tank, grinding closer and closer.

The General whooped with glee.

'Fire, fire!' he cried, hitting the red button again.

The jet of water shot out faster and faster from the toy gun, washing Master Goldtail and his mice across the floor.

'Stop!' the Chief Constable cried. 'Stop firing and let me arrest them!'

But the thieves were being swept closer and closer to the garden door, until eventually the water sprayed them on to the doormat.

They finally managed to scramble upright, clinging to the rough matting. 'Run!' Master Goldtail cried. 'Run for your lives!' And with the water blasting at their heels, all four mice fled under the door in terror.

'Stop them!' the Chief Constable cried.

He darted for the hatch, and pressed it open. 'Come on, let's get them!' he shouted.

He was about to fling himself outside, but then suddenly there was a bright glare. The kitchen lights had come on. The Chief Constable ducked back inside. And when the mice peered out through the sherbet-smudged windscreen they got the most terrible fright:

Arthur and Lucy had appeared!

Chapter Fifteen

Arthur stared at the toy tank in astonishment. 'How did that get here?' he said. 'I left it in the drawing room!'

Tumtum and the others looked at each other in horror. If Arthur opened the hatch of the tank, he was sure to find them.

But then the children heard a strange noise, like an engine revving, and next moment they saw

a light flicker under the garden door.

They ran and opened it, and when they saw outside they both gasped. For there was the toy bus, clattering up the garden path!

'Catch it!' Arthur cried, stumbling on to the doorstep.

Lucy grabbed the torch from the shelf and ran after him. And as the children rushed into the garden, Tumtum and the others slithered out of the tank and crept under the dresser.

They could hear the toy bus clattering down the path, and the children chasing after it.

'Stop!' Arthur shouted – but the bus was going at a cracking pace. Master Goldtail was driving it as fast as it would go, speeding towards a gap in the hedge.

'Faster, faster!' the clowns all shrieked, looking through the back windscreen in terror. But the children were catching up with them. And just as the bus was swerving on to the lawn, a huge pink hand appeared in the headlights, and clamped over the windscreen.

And when the mice looked in the wing mirror, they saw Arthur unhitching the wagons from behind them. Then the bus was lifted high into the air.

They pushed on the doors, desperately trying to get out. But Arthur had shut the catches on the outside. They were locked in.

'Put us down!' cried Mr Moody.

'*Let us go!*' roared Master Goldtail, thumping the window with rage.

The children shone their torch into the bus in amazement.

'It must be Master Goldtail and his gang!' Lucy said. 'And look, they're even wearing circus clothes!'

Arthur and Lucy had met some very strange mice before. Even so, they were rather astonished.

'Aren't they extraordinary!' Lucy said. 'I say, do you think it was *them* who broke into the village shop? Nutmeg said they were very wicked – so breaking into a village shop is just the sort of thing they might do!'

'Let's look in the wagons,' Arthur said. 'If they did raid the shop, then we'll probably find some of the things they stole.'

They carefully carried the bus and the wagons

back into the kitchen, and set them down on the table.

Tumtum and the others watched excitedly from under the dresser. Then Nutmeg and Mrs Marchmouse heard the commotion, and came running out too.

'Oh, thank goodness you're all right,' Nutmeg cried, clutching Tumtum's paw. 'But you're soaked! Whatever's been going on?'

'Shh!' Tumtum said, pointing into the kitchen. 'The children have caught Goldtail and his gang! They all tried to drive off in the toy bus, but Arthur and Lucy chased after them, and now they've locked them in!'

'Oh, how clever of them!' Nutmeg said proudly.

They all crouched very still, watching as the

children searched the wagons.

When they opened the door of the first wagon, a beetle bounced out.

'Eugh!' said Lucy, stepping back in fright. The beetle scuttled about the table, then hopped to the floor and disappeared under the sink.

The next wagon was full of tiny cardboard boxes, sealed with brown tape. Arthur took out his penknife, and carefully slit them open. When the children saw what they contained, they both gasped.

For each box was full of the tiniest, most exquisite treasures – gold plates and jugs, and candlesticks, and paintings and tapestries; all mouse-sized.

'These must be all the things they stole from

other mice's mouse-holes,' Lucy said, spreading everything out on the table. 'We shall have to give them all to Nutmeg. I'm sure she can find out which mice they belong to, and give them all back!'

The next three wagons were furnished with bunk beds and dressing tables, and wardrobes containing tiny suits of clothes. And the last wagon was full of tubes of sherbet!

'Look!' Arthur said. 'This must be the sherbet that was stolen from the village shop!' He reached into the wagon, and pulled out one of the tubes. It had scuffs at the end, where it had been nibbled. 'Goodness,' he said. 'Just think how astonished Mrs Paterson will be when she learns that the robbers were mice!'

Master Goldtail and the clowns could not bear to see their loot being touched. They beat the windows so hard that the bus started to shake.

'They're going to get out!' Arthur said anxiously. 'Quick, let's get Pa. He'll know what to do with them!'

Lucy ran upstairs. Mr Mildew was in his study, struggling with his latest invention – a mechanical pencil that could write and spell all by itself. He hardly looked up when Lucy came in. 'What is it?' he muttered. 'Didn't I say you were meant to stay in your room?'

'Oh, yes, but please come downstairs – we've got something to show you,' Lucy said. 'Oh please come and see, then you'll understand everything!'

Mr Mildew grudgingly followed her

downstairs. But when he saw what was on the kitchen table, his eyes bulged in astonishment.

'By Jove!' he exclaimed.

'They're the ones who robbed the shop,' Lucy said. 'Look! Here's all the sherbet they took!'

Mr Mildew hardly knew what to say. 'I had better call Mrs Paterson,' he said. He picked up the telephone, and in a trembling voice told her to come at once.

She hurried to Rose Cottage, wondering what could have happened. And when she saw the mice scrabbling about in the toy bus, and the stolen sherbet, she was too astonished to speak.

It took two strong cups of tea to stop her shaking.

'What are we going to do with them?' Mr

Mildew asked, fearing the children might want to keep them as pets.

'Oh, we don't want them at Rose Cottage,' Lucy said. 'They're too noisy!'

'Perhaps we could find a cage for them, and keep them in the garden shed, where we wouldn't have to look at them all the time,' Arthur said.

'*A garden shed!* How dare you!' Master Goldtail shouted, not liking the sound of this one bit.

'Oh, stop squealing!' Arthur said, rapping the bus with a spoon.

'They would be wasted in a shed!' Mrs Paterson said, gathering her wits again. 'They are MUCH too good for that. If you don't want them, I shall sell them for you at the village shop! I'll put

an advertisement in the local newspaper, and sell them to whoever offers the most money! I'm sure they'll fetch a *fortune*. Four mice dressed in funny clothes, breaking into my shop, and driving off in a toy bus . . . They must be the cleverest mice in the whole wide world! Why, I shouldn't be surprised if they don't become stars on the television!'

'Oh, what a good idea!' Lucy cried.

'And I shall give all the money to you,' Mrs Paterson said kindly. 'And you can keep the sherbet too! It's the least you deserve. I am sorry about this morning, my dears. It was quite wrong of me to accuse you of stealing.'

'Oh, don't worry about that,' Lucy said. This morning seemed like ages ago – they were just glad things had turned out so well.

'I'll take them with me now,' Mrs Paterson said, tucking the bus firmly under her arm. 'I've a nice big cage back at home I can put them in – it's one my niece used to use for her gerbils. Then I'll give your bus a good clean, and bring it back to you in the morning, along with that poor old toy policeman, of course!'

Everyone laughed – and they didn't notice that the prisoners had become quiet. 'The telly, just think of that!' Mr Moody whispered. 'We'll be famous!'

'And rich!' Mr Mirth tittered.

'Sounds better than driving round in a flea-bitten old circus!' Mr Merry said.

In his mind's eye, Master Goldtail suddenly had a delicious image of himself dressed in dark

glasses, being chauffeured between television studios in the back of a sleek limousine – and he decided things hadn't turned out so badly after all.

Tumtum and the others all cheered when Mrs Paterson carried the thieves away.

'I shall telephone *The Mouse Times* first thing in the morning, and tell them the burglars have been caught, and that it was all thanks to me – er, us!' the General said boastfully.

'And tomorrow I shall go round all the local mouse-holes, returning the stolen goods to their rightful owners,' the Chief Constable said happily. 'Just think how pleased they shall all be!'

They hid under the dresser, waiting until Mr Mildew and the children had gone upstairs. 'I shall go up to the attic tonight, and write the children a letter, congratulating them on everything they've done,' Nutmeg said. 'And I shall tell them to keep the wagons. They belong to Arthur's circus now!'

Everyone agreed. 'And now let's have a celebration!' Tumtum said, leading them all back to Nutmouse Hall. 'Have we anything to eat, dear?' he asked Nutmeg anxiously. 'I feel quite hollow!'

'Why, of course!' Nutmeg replied. 'We've got the General's birthday feast! The table's still laid in the banqueting room, and the cake hasn't been touched!'

They all cheered. After such a grand adventure, a feast was just what they needed. Tumtum set two extra places for Mrs Marchmouse and the Chief Constable, and soon they were all sitting down at

the big oak table, feasting long into the night.

The birthday party was two days late, but all the better for it. The candles flickered and the champagne flowed, and by the time Nutmeg carried in the cake, everyone had quite forgotten how badly the General had behaved.

'*Happy Birthday to you! Happy Birthday to you! Happy Birthday dear Gen – er – al . . . Happy Birthday to you!*' they all sang, thumping their silver teaspoons on the table.

The General glowed. What a wonderful adventure it had turned out to be! And just think what a hero he would be when he told *The Mouse Times* how he had chased Master Goldtail from Nutmouse Hall in a toy tank!

'*For I'm a jolly good fellow!*' he sang, blowing

out his candles with a single puff. And the mood was so merry, even the Chief Constable agreed that a better General there never was.

Arthur and Lucy clambered into bed in the attic, unaware of the festivities going on downstairs. They had left Nutmeg a letter on the chest of drawers, telling her everything that had happened – for they could little have guessed that she had been watching from beneath the dresser.

'Arthur,' Lucy asked hesitantly. 'I was just thinking, and I know it's strange but . . . well, we've had so many funny adventures with mice, you don't think *Nutmeg* might be a mouse, do you?'

Nutmeg had told them in a letter that she was a Fairy of Sorts, and the children had always

accepted this. But now Lucy was starting to have her doubts.

'I suppose it's possible,' Arthur said sleepily. 'Well, she's sure to come up here tonight and fetch the letter. Let's take it in turns to stay awake, and watch the chest of drawers!'

'All right,' Lucy said. 'I'll keep watch first, then I'll wake you up at midnight, and you can take over.'

Arthur muttered his agreement, and quickly fell asleep. Lucy propped herself up on her pillow, watching the moon slip through the curtains. It was very exciting to think she might finally find out who Nutmeg was. But an hour passed, and then another, and her eyes got heavier and heavier . . . and by the time Nutmeg finally crept upstairs, Lucy

was far away, dreaming of mice dressed as clowns, and of fairies with long, nutmeg tails.

EGMONT PRESS: ETHICAL PUBLISHING

Egmont Press is about turning writers into successful authors and children into passionate readers – producing books that enrich and entertain. As a responsible children's publisher, we go even further, considering the world in which our consumers are growing up.

Safety First
Naturally, all of our books meet legal safety requirements. But we go further than this; every book with play value is tested to the highest standards – if it fails, it's back to the drawing-board.

Made Fairly
We are working to ensure that the workers involved in our supply chain – the people that make our books – are treated with fairness and respect.

Responsible Forestry
We are committed to ensuring all our papers come from environmentally and socially responsible forest sources.

For more information, please visit our website at www.egmont.co.uk/ethical